Rx FOR RECIDIVISM

Barbara H Mullen Reed, EdD

Rx For Recidivism

Book design by Barbara H Mullen Reed, EdD
Back Page Author Photograph: Barbara H Mullen Reed, EdD

This is a Work of Fiction
Written by Barbara H Mullen Reed, EdD

Visit my website at barbarareedauthor.com
Printed in the United States of America
First Printing: September 2017
Published by: Sojourn Publishing, LLC

ISBN: 978-1-62747-146-6
Ebook ISBN: 978-1-62747-148-0

"Woe to those who plan iniquity, to those who plot evil on their beds! At morning's light, they carry it out because it is in their power to do it." ~Micah 2:1

"The trade in human beings, a modern form of slavery … violates the God-given dignity of so many of our brothers and sisters and constitutes a true crime against humanity." ~Pope Francis

"Practice random acts of beauty and senseless acts of love." ~ unknown

Foreword

At the time of the initial research for this book, in the 1970s, the practice was that 16-18-year- old young men who were classified as having committed crimes fitting certain categories and who had been found guilty of the charges, would be thoroughly screened by the local probation department in the jurisdiction in which the criminal act occurred. Each probation report covered the subject's IQ, the work and school history, the family dynamic, the religious practice, the criminal history of the young man, and a summary of the interviews that had substantiated the data.

The probation report was a crucial aspect of the adjudication process. The report contained specific recommendations by the probation officer as to disposition of the offender whom the Court had adjudged to be guilty and to be a felony offender. The reports containing the sentencing recommendations were signed: *Respectfully Submitted,* followed by the signature of the probation officer assigned to each case.

Prior to the advent of computer technology and photocopy machines, these probation reports would be typed and copies made using carbon paper and thin paper known as "onionskin." The original would be forwarded to the Court and the copy would be placed in a file folder with other items, such as copies of any medical reports and the individual's "rap" sheet, which contained his fingerprints and basic background information such as full name, any known aliases, date and place of birth, marital status, religion, date and place and details of the alleged crime, listing of prior offenses and sentences, and a photo taken at the time of finger printing. At several points along the way, the file could easily be slipped out of the container in which it was housed or pages could be removed. This was an unusual occurrence, but it did happen. When it did, the fate of the subject of the investigation could take an unexpected turn. This created an opening for such anomalies as men allegedly of impeccable backgrounds seeking to adopt or to "sponsor" teenage boys to intervene and to offer to provide a "service to the community."

Once the sentence had been imposed and the offender was in prison or on probation, the files were stored. Storage of the files was also a problem, as space was limited. Copies of the files became a burden to the county court house personnel of the facility where they were housed. The solution at that time was (after a period of a year or two) to pile them into garbage cans and send them off to be strewn about the county landfill. This was before the invention of paper shredders.

Through this unusual (by present day standards) system of compilation and disposal of vital records, I had the good fortune one day, about thirty-five years ago, to receive a telephone call from a lawyer who was at a courthouse in New York State and noticed that several boxes of these files were about to dumped into the trash. He knew I had recently completed a doctoral dissertation for which the topic was recidivism among 16- 18-year-old felony offenders who had been sentenced to prison terms in medium and maximum secure prisons and who had resided in rural counties in upstate New York. The lawyer stated that if I would like to have those "old" files from the courthouse basement, I should drive down immediately, and the maintenance staff would be happy to dispose of them by loading them into my car.

I don't believe I have ever been presented with a greater gift. I received grateful thanks from the courthouse staff for relieving them of the "burden" of these files from the 1960s, and I drove away with data that was invaluable to me as a researcher. I immediately redacted names and Social Security numbers, (a precaution that would not have been accomplished had the records been disposed of in the usual manner), and prepared a brief study based on the IQ scores, level of education, and reading achievement scores of the subjects. After that, I put the files away and awaited the time when my family and professional demands might ease, and I would have time to write something for posterity that would advance the cause of rehabilitation of young felony offenders. And so it is, that in 2017 I find myself writing the story that actually began so many years ago, but is so timely today. The question remains: What is the most effective way to make a positive change in the lives of 16- 18-year-old young men who are found guilty of serious crimes?

The subjects of the files I was given and those who are performing in this present fictionalized account, did not grow up in violent neighborhoods in large cities. They were from rural areas where family farms and small businesses still flourished. They were from families in which parents struggled to survive financially and usually had left school by the time they would have been in the 8th grade. Their children repeated this pattern.

These are families rarely included in sociological studies. Their lives are so unremarkable, in contrast to the high drama and spectacular crimes that are happening in the large cities, that they receive little publicity. They are often the forgotten parents and children. They do not acclimate well to prison life, or to the alternative of probation that returns them immediately to an unstable home life. The result is twofold: if they are released on probation, the lack of a family and community support system almost guarantees a repeat offense. Or, after serving the traumatic months of a prison sentence, they leave prison ill prepared for the return to their unstructured lives on the outside. The cycle repeats, and they often become lifelong casualties of "the system."

Over the years, I have seen instances of exploitation of the naiveté and inexperience of these young people. The reality of their circumstances can be harsh, and I believe their story must at last be told.

Rather than continuing to prescribe institutional remedies that are almost certain to be a prescription for a return to a life of increased criminal activity, it is time to break the cycle and implement instead an "Rx for Rehabilitation."

Introduction

Rehabilitation of prisoners has been an ongoing topic of lively discussion in the United States over a period of many years. Prior to the Industrial Revolution, prisons as we know them, did not exist in our country. Persons committing offenses were held in jail for a very short time until their punishment could be determined. Public execution by burning or hanging, public shaming by placing the person in stocks, or in a birdcage device with sharp spikes, etc. were some of the punishments of choice. Public beatings and whippings also were popular. If a person died in the course of public punishment, it was considered to be God's plan.

In 1790 the first federal penitentiary was opened in Philadelphia. The name reflects the purpose. Convicted persons were placed there solely to reflect, in isolation and in total silence, on their misdeeds and to "repent." Release followed repentance. Unfortunately, prisoners were more likely to have mental and physical breakdowns than to reform.

Our present idea of using the captive prison population as an unpaid workforce arose during the Industrial Revolution. The theory was that the silent inmates could reflect on their misdeeds while turning out manufactured products. Absent the practice of isolation, the entrepreneurs had discovered a lucrative solution to the prison problem. The prisoners adapted well to the more active life, and by 1819 prisons had sprung up all over the country using this model. Prisons became self-supporting by selling the items manufactured by the unpaid inmate workforce.

The 1900s brought opposition by labor unions to this masterful system of manufacturing. Legislation was passed greatly restricting the sale of goods produced in the prisons, as businesses on the "outside" could not compete with the prices for which prison goods were sold. It became more difficult to fund job training and educational programs in the prisons as the 20th century progressed. Looking at the situation in the present day, it is apparent that there is now and has been for the past fifty years much need for prison reform and to alternatives to punishment by incarceration.

Overcrowding has led to some questionable practices that seem to have turned the prisons into hostile, armed camps in which inmates are feared and controlled by any means necessary. In the late 1970s, when I spent four years working from an office in one of the most effectively run prisons in which 16- 18-year-old felony prisoners were incarcerated, the constant level of noise in the cell blocks was almost unbearable. Inmates screamed and pounded on the bars of the tiered cellblocks. Visits to similar facilities in the state produced comparable results. In the classrooms, many of the prisoners stood on the desks and were generally disruptive. According to the records I was reviewing at the time, almost 100% of the prisoners were medicated to make them more manageable. The prison personnel were genuinely caring people in almost all instances, but they were not given programs and materials appropriate to the needs of the population. There was also no program in place (other than medication) to address the overwhelming mental-health challenges. There was no program tailored to students with learning disabilities.

Because of the fear that "gangs and cliques" would form, a process called "churning" was put in place at that time. A young man would be tested upon entry and would be placed, for example, in a program where he might be taught basic carpentry skills. Within three months, he would be rotated out of that program and sent to another prison facility where he would be retested and some weeks later placed in a program which might bear no relation to the one to which he had been previously assigned. Chaos was the operative mode. All too often, tamping down the chaos was the treatment modality.

The fictional account presented here examines several settings, other than prison, of coping with young men who commit crimes. I have personally witnessed each of these modalities. However, the narrative and its characters are products of the author's imagination.

The first involves a privileged youth named Sid Harkness. Sid emerges in the early chapters as a shadowy, somewhat sinister figure. He refuses to be ignored and moves to center stage in Part II. Sid grew up in an atmosphere of education and culture. The setting in which Sid's parents meet and in which Sid spends his formative years, is in my much loved hometown of Ithaca, New York and on its Cornell University campus. As stated earlier, all characters and their activities, as depicted in the book, are pure fiction.

As Sid matures, he kills more than once without consequences, and attracts to himself a group of wealthy, unscrupulous people who exploit children and consider themselves above the law. Together, they devise a method of dealing with teenaged boys who have committed crimes that provides the offenders with a life of luxury that brings wealth to the sponsors with no cost to the taxpayers or the State. It also eliminates recidivism, as the boys do not survive.

The second group, represented by Jeremy Cook, are boys, often with great potential, who are caught up in a culture of lack and of neglect and have begun to steal and to enter the criminal justice system marked as teenaged felons. They are vulnerable and inexperienced and are ideal subjects for exploitation by the first group. Whether released on probation or on parole after time served in prison, in almost every instance, they go on to commit additional crimes and enter the statistical database as recidivists.

The third group is represented by Jess Sampson, his wife Allison, and their parents. They are grounded, loving, savvy people who are led to become aware of and to truly understand the problem, and to responsibly construct meaningful and lasting alternative solutions. Their transformative process is included in its entirety in Parts I and III, as it illustrates the great hope that people who are kind, compassionate, and skilled as parents and teachers, will begin to recognize and to nurture the many "Jeremys" among us. Their rehabilitation program eliminates repeat offenses in almost all cases, and achieves the success that responsible public officials, educators, and family members strive for.

In Part III, the three groups are brought together through a series of events that profoundly influence each of their lives, individually and collectively. The focus of Part III is the rescue and rehabilitation of Jeremy whose life has been touched by both Sid and Jess. The intent is to bring a just and lasting resolution to the problems encountered by the young men who have criminal records and by those who seek solutions.

There is violence, and there is sexually explicit language. This raw material, the fabric of the stark reality of the fictional scenarios depicted, reflects actual events, and such details have not been softened or omitted.

Barbara H Reed, EdD
2017

Contents

PART I

JESS

Chapter One
Hint of Danger, 1996

On a sunny mid-April morning in 1996, Jess Sampson was sitting happily at his drafting board working on the detail of an architectural drawing of the front elevation of a large home. The sunlight from the front picture window fell across his face, filtered to a gentle glow by the solar screen shades. It accented his slightly tousled blond hair, his friendly sky-blue eyes and the generous lips that always seemed to be just about ready to open in a wide grin. A Vanessa Williams CD played softly in the background. There was the faint scent of cinnamon in the air.

"Hello," he said into the phone, "This is Jess..."

"Oh, Hi Mom. What's happening?"

As he stood and moved over to sit in his favorite easy chair, Jess could picture his mother, Mary Sampson, smiling (she seemed to always be happy and, like Florida, mostly sunny). She would be sitting with her feet up in her favorite blue-leather recliner on the lanai of their little condo in Sarasota, Florida. Her toenails would sparkle through the open-toed sandals that she wore around the house. She would have painted the toenails with her favorite rose-glow polish, but only the toenails. She said that it wore off too fast from her fingers when she did housework. She liked to be free to clean, and cook, and do gardening without worrying about chipped fingernail paint. Her formerly tinted blonde hair had turned to a salt and pepper color, and she wore it in bouncy, shoulder-length curls she styled herself from a Toni home permanent kit. She would be wearing an apron over her T-shirt and shorts and would be ready to jump up at any minute to prepare lunch or a snack for Dad. They had probably already been to the beach early that morning to take a long walk and look for shells.

Wade Sampson was tall and muscular with a trim figure and permanent laugh lines around his mouth and eyes. He preferred to have his thick gray hair styled in a maintenance-free brush cut. He loved life, and he loved his wife. They had fun every day just being together. They worked on the lawn and the flower and vegetable beds, pruned and planted fruit trees, went to the beach, played bridge with the neighbors once a week, went to the Asolo Theater to see plays, attended the little Episcopal Mission Church that was rapidly growing into a full-fledged parish, and spent a lot of time just relaxing and talking on the lanai. Every day they went to the Y to exercise, and they did water aerobics in a class twice a week. Jess was happy that his parents had such a fulfilling life and thrilled they were healthy and able to be so active in retirement. They had given him a wonderful upbringing, and he hoped that they would have these years to celebrate being with each other.

"We were just talking about you," Mary's voice drifted into his daydreaming. "What exciting new building projects do you have going?"

"I have a few," Jess answered with a grin. "I have been asked to design and engineer the building of ten custom homes near Falls Church. It's a complicated project because of the way the lots are designed. Each one is five acres and they all back up to a nature preserve. As I've said in the past, the idea of a 'nature preserve' isn't always the same for the seller and the developer. It may mean that the preserved land is impossible to drain properly and is really swamp land. There may have been questionable fill brought in and plowed into the buildable portion of the area. I've looked this piece of land over really carefully and studied the history of it. I'm convinced that it's a real prize."

"That sounds like a fantastic project!" Mary chimed in. "Will the houses be secluded or out in the open looking at each other?"

Jess chuckled. "It's sort of a semicircle. Each lot is bordered by really beautiful woods on three sides at the moment. That may have to be changed based on the size of the house. I haven't found any huge boulders anywhere yet. It seems to drain well after a heavy storm. Of course, it has that heavy Virginia red clay soil, and whoever does the landscaping will have to haul in and spread a lot of quality top soil.

"I'm working on the drawings of the front elevations and the positioning of the different styles on the plat plan. There will be some flexibility in the design of each home, but each one must enhance the overall look and feel of the place. It will be essential to stick to that premise. These will be in the million-dollar range and up. Buyers in that price range can be insistent in wanting certain amenities, styles, trim, roof colors, and building materials. We'll just have to be firm in our resolve to make each home compatible but unique from the others. I can't wait to get final approval on the plat plan so I can start advertising and working with real estate agents and buyers!"

"I know you'll do well, son," she said. "You have an instinct for this sort of thing. I knew from the minute you started in on Lincoln logs and Erector sets that you would design buildings. And here you are!

"Oh, here comes Dad."

She handed the phone to Wade and his deep voice greeted Jess. "Do you remember when you were here last and there were beef cattle just across the fence in our back yard?"

"Sure."

"Well they sold the farm and they're building a whole forest of little houses there. They're widening the road out front, too. Is this supposed to be progress, or should we be upset?"

Jess laughed and felt the lines around his own mouth and eyes crinkle like those of his Dad. "You can be upset, but it's going to happen anyway, so you might as well think of it as 'fine tuning.' You have a great little circle of homes on your cul de sac and it just wasn't meant to stay farmland in your back yard. The good news is that your circle is a couple blocks back from that main road that they're widening, so you won't lose any frontage and you won't be anywhere near the road noise. I'd say, keep smiling and celebrate the fact that you're in a highly desirable area where property values will be on the rise!"

"That's how I look at it too," his Dad chuckled.

"When can you come to Virginia for a visit?" Jess asked. "I can send you a plane ticket any time, and as you know, I've got lots of room in this beautiful house. I'd love to have your company!" Can you take a couple weeks off and come on up?"

"We miss you, Jess, and I think it's a great idea. Mom and I'll talk it over tonight. The idea of a couple weeks in Virginia sounds tempting! I'll call you back tomorrow morning and we'll look over some dates on the calendar meanwhile."

"Sounds good, Dad. I miss you and Mom too! Give each other a hug for me!"

They all said goodbye to each other, and Jess started back to work.

But the phone rang again. This time the caller was Sid Harkness.

Sid was a mortgage broker in Fairfax County, Virginia whose company had handled a number of loans for Jess's home buyers. Jess could picture the caller's brooding eyes and dark, intense gaze as he listened to his request. He thought of Sid's face, with one eye that seemed to be off kilter. Sid almost always had that dark, almost sinister look and often peeked out at the world scowling under heavy black brows and lashes. Sid never looked anyone in the eye, in fact he seemed to have something wrong with his eye. He rubbed his right eye a lot as if trying to see clearly.

Sid was withdrawn and somehow hostile even when he was smiling his strange, detached smile. He was tall and husky in build and sort of ruggedly handsome in a rough way, the way a pirate captain is in an action movie.

Right now, on the phone, Sid was trying to keep it off-hand and sincere, but Jess sensed an urgency that couldn't be hidden. Sid was calling his casual business associate, Jess, to ask a rather unusual favor.

"Listen, Jess, I'm tied up in a meeting that's showing signs of going on for at least two more hours. I feel funny asking you this, but could you possibly pick up my nephew, Jeremy, from high school and drop him off at my apartment? He'll be fine on his own, but he does need a ride home."

Jess was puzzled at the sudden personal request being made of him by this man he knew only from business interactions. Jess thought of the vague rumor he had heard about Sid. It was rumored that Sid had been responsible for the fatal accident that had killed the founder of the business of which Sid was now the owner and director. "Stop that!" Jess told himself. "This man is a successful businessman… and probably a person of good character." But, he didn't really believe that.

There was something about Sid that was definitely giving off warning signals to him. He decided to take a chance, though. It couldn't do any harm to give the nephew a ride home from school that day.

"Sure," Jess replied without hesitation. "Just give me the time and the address of the school and the apartment. I'm pretty much finished early for once, and I'll be glad to do it."

"I'll call the school and have them give Jeremy a message that you'll pick him up so he can watch for you. What make of car will you be driving?"

"It's an SUV, a silver Honda Passport, 1995."

"OK." Sid gave the instructions, and when he was finished, abruptly hung up the phone.

At the school, Jess was able to recognize Jeremy easily from the description Sid had provided. Jeremy came out walking alone. He had a mop of blond hair and was tall and slender. He was neatly dressed in chinos, a dress shirt and a sweater. His shoes were tan leather topsiders. This seemed to be a kind of school "uniform" as the other boys coming out of the building were similarly dressed. He walked with his eyes averted, but Jess could tell he had spotted the car. Jess got out and stood beside the passenger door, and put out his hand. Jeremy kept his eyes on the door rather than on Jess, but he gave a shy smile as they shook hands. Jess saw that his eyes were a clear, very bright blue. They looked sad. Jeremy hopped in the car and gave directions to the apartment house, which was about five miles away.

As they drove, Jess asked what subjects Jeremy liked best, if he played any sports … the usual general-interest questions designed to put him at ease. Jeremy replied politely, but was guarded and did not look at Jess as he answered. It seemed from his monosyllabic answers that he liked math best, that he had an interest in history and geography and that he exercised regularly in the gym, shot baskets, but did not play any sports as part of a team. He did say he liked to watch basketball games and that he followed some of the college teams.

The apartment house was in an upscale neighborhood, and it looked to be exclusive. Jeremy got out of the car, muttered a polite "Thank you," then turned toward the brass plated front doors. A doorman let Jeremy in. Jeremy did not turn to wave goodbye, but seemed to be focused on getting inside.

After that, there were a series of calls, about one every three weeks, always from Sid, in which he asked for the same favor. Jess casually asked Jeremy on one of the school-to-home "shuttles" if Sid had many meetings. Jeremy replied that recently Sid was away at meetings most nights and did not return home until about 6:00AM. He added that Sid usually picked him up at school and dropped him off at home before he left for those all night meetings. Sid always took Jeremy to school in the mornings.

Jess's uneasiness about Sid grew after that revelation. Jeremy and Jess got to know each other a little and a couple times Jess stopped at a fast-food restaurant and bought food Jeremy said he would like to eat while he did his homework that night.

Jess never went into the apartment house, but he assumed it was an upscale living space, as the apartment building was quite grand in design and was at a prestigious address. He and Jeremy would chat on the way from school about Jeremy's high-school subjects and his interest in basketball. Nothing personal was ever discussed, and Sid was seldom mentioned.

As the calls continued, Jess began to wonder why Jeremy's uncle was spending so much time away from the boy. The thought was creeping into his mind that the relationship between Sid and his nephew was not a happy one, and that it could be even more troubling than that. He casually asked a colleague about Sid and was dismayed to hear that Sid had a reputation for some business dealings that were ethically questionable. There was also that rumor that had floated around, but had never been substantiated, that Sid had killed at least one person. He was a man to keep at a distance, Jess decided. That left a major concern that was bothering him more and more. What, if anything, should he do about Jeremy? He genuinely liked the boy, and he had a nagging fear that Jeremy was somehow in danger.

One night in late August, Jess dreamed of his wife, Allison, as he often did. It was sometimes hard to recapture the dreams after he woke, but that night the dream was so vivid it seemed real. In it, Allison came to him as a feeling, a presence, accompanied by the absolute assurance that she was really there. He could actually feel the air moving and recognized the energy field that he knew to be hers. He was still asleep, or at least it felt like he was asleep, but he recognized the sensation of her smoothing his hair. It was as if his hand was on hers. He was only half asleep as he realized that his hand was moving over his hair but that he could feel her hand under his, somehow moving it along.

"Allison, Allison I love you so much."

Allison was trying to tell him something urgently. He was drifting back into sleep and was clearly seeing an image of Sid now. Sid, glowering and threatening. Sid was looking absolutely menacing. Jeremy came floating into the dream from somewhere, looking confused and sad. Sid lunged in Jeremy's direction with his hands that now had swords growing out of them. A wave of Allison's calm and beautiful energy came forward and rested beside him again, and somehow Jess understood that she wanted him to protect Jeremy from something closely connected to Sid. "I will, Sweetheart, he murmured. "I'll look after Jeremy."

During a break at the office the next day, Jess decided to take the opportunity to get on his laptop and try to find out more about the mysterious Sid Harkness.

A quick search revealed a reference to a news article about the sudden death in 1985 of a man named Albert Fisher who had been the founder of Community Corners Mortgage, a highly successful mortgage company in the Rockville, Maryland area. Fisher had been found dead in his Mercedes automobile at a remote Catoctin Mountain camping area. The death had eventually been ruled a suicide.

An earlier article mentioned there had been extensive questioning of a director of the company named Sidney A. Harkness as to the circumstances of the death of Albert Fisher. Harkness was able to establish an alibi that removed him from any geographic connection to the deceased at the time of the tragic event. It was noted that Harkness had been named the successor to Fisher and according to the terms of an irrevocable trust established by Fisher just prior to his death, had inherited the business and the building in Rockville in which it was located.

This was the source of the rumor Jess had heard about Sid. There was much more to Sid than appeared on the surface. Again, the danger signals nagged at Jess. He had to be watchful. He felt a responsibility for Jeremy now. He would have to wait for and seize the moment when it came that would lead him to the heart of the mystery. From there, he would find the path that would direct him toward the best possible outcome for Jeremy.

Chapter Two
Looking Back Ten Years
Jess, 1986

Just as the sun was setting, Jess opened the exit door of his work place and glimpsed it disappearing behind the building across the way. The sky was streaked with bands of glorious purples and yellows as the light source slipped away. It was a metaphor for his young adult life. Jess had been a serious student, deemed by his teachers to be destined for great things – maybe a foreign diplomat with his facility for learning other languages, or a leader in government or a designer of buildings. That had been the prediction. Yet here he was at age 28, a graduate of Cornell University with a bachelor's degree in Engineering and a master's in architecture, employed at a start-up company on the beltway in Maryland programming computers. It was 1986, and his annual salary was $25,000.

He was renting one room in a mansion in Potomac from a divorcee who had a teenaged son in boarding school in New England. The woman dated almost every night but did not entertain at home. This made for privacy for Jess and a quiet, too quiet, life. He wasn't a television viewer, so he read most nights and was asleep by 9:00 p.m. His landlady left him alone and gave him the run of the house. He prepared his own simple meals and left everything neat and orderly. He sometimes had little discussions with himself about how boring his life was becoming.

This all changed when a co-worker asked if he would be interested in teaching a computer course, two nights a week at Montgomery College in Rockville. "Why not," Jess replied. He went for an interview after work and began teaching a few weeks later, at the start of the fall semester.

The change in Jess's routine produced immediate results. He began to spend time at the college computer lab on some of the evenings that he was not teaching in order to be better prepared. He was energized by the presence of the eager young computer users who kept him challenged with their questions and their intuitive knowledge of how to interact with the complex machines. With this added stimulus, his class moved quickly from the basics to advanced areas of programming.

A number of students wanted to start a Computer Club. They insisted that Jess be the club's advisor. He thought it would be an informal group, but the students went to the Dean of Students and arranged for it to be an official college-sponsored club and for Jess to be formally appointed its advisor. This brought him an additional stipend and gave him access to a wide range of resources. Jess would have been happy to guide the club as a volunteer. He was learning as much from the students as they were from him.

The club met on Friday evenings in the computer lab. That was a time when few classes or other groups were on campus. Parking was wide open. The campus may have been quiet, but the enthusiasm in the lab was at a high level. Through an arrangement with Apple and with IBM, the lab was outfitted with the latest technology. The Tandy and Apple IIs had been around for a while. The IBM Peanut had just come on the scene. The rapidly advancing technology was keeping the students engaged and discussions were lively. Computer gaming was developing by leaps and bounds. This not only involved fascinating programming challenges, but also required the right accompanying music to make the game a hit!

The Club attracted students representing all age groups from teenagers to senior citizens, and the number of women was equal to that of men. Jess had been enjoying his role in the Computer Club for almost a year when his life suddenly changed. One Friday evening just before Winter break, a student named Carol Lewis brought her friend Allison to the Club. Jess first saw Allison at a computer when he turned from helping a student named Kurt, in the first row, with an algorithm. As he suddenly found himself looking into Allison's hazel eyes, he imagined his heart, or was it his mind, performing a totally unfamiliar flip flop maneuver. Allison had curly black hair that shone in the light and cascaded down her back in ringlets. Her face was so startlingly beautiful that he saw light radiating from it. Friends later remarked at her plainness, but to him, she was the embodiment of a light such as he had never seen. He watched in awe as her delicate fingers flew over the computer keys in perfect synchronicity. She continued typing as she glanced at him, never missing a beat. Her perfectly formed lips parted in a little smile. He felt a sudden burst of heat fill his body, and he wondered if he was staring at her.

Carol came to the rescue. She saw Jess standing there and introduced Allison to him. Allison gracefully stood and extended her hand. He saw that she was tall and willowy, about two inches shorter than his lanky six-foot frame. As Jess took her hand in both of his, and looked slightly downward into those amazing eyes, he felt another jolt of heat. He had never before experienced this sensation in any of his encounters – with women or for that matter, with men. All he could think of was that he had to meet this woman again and that there would be a month of winter break following this class. This was the moment if there was to be one. Allison, meanwhile, was looking at Jess and feeling some of the same sensations as he. She looked up into the blazing blue eyes and noticed how friendly and kind they were. She quickly took in the mop of unruly blond, curly hair, and the genuine, gentle smile. She had to set aside a sudden impulse to hug him.

Frantically, with as much calm as he could muster, Jess spoke. "I'd like to talk with you during the Winter break. If you'll be in town, could we meet next week for coffee?"

Allison replied immediately, while trying to regain her composure, but without even considering the question, "I would be able to meet on Tuesday after work. Would that be good for you?"

Jess felt his mouth go dry. He was not used to being speechless in his well-ordered life. "Tuesday would be perfect. How about dinner? I get back from work around 6:00, and we could meet at Chopstix at 7:00 if you like that time," he stammered, "that is, if you like Chinese food."

Allison smiled her brilliant smile and accepted. Reluctantly, Jess moved around the room to other students.

He was never the same again.

Chapter Three
Loving Allison 1986

Jess and Allison met at the newly opened Chop Stix Restaurant as planned. They were seated at a table and given menus, but neither of them opened them. They just sat and smiled at each other. Allison looked into his eyes and spoke in her soft, gentle voice, "Wow!" Jess tried to speak, but he couldn't. Here he was, the teacher who was never at a loss for words, and he was speechless. He nodded and reached across the small table and took her hands in his. They were soft and warm. She closed her fingers around his, and he would have been content to stay just like that forever.

Finally, he found the words, "It's as if I have been searching for you forever," he said. He could barely speak above a whisper and had no idea why he was daring to saying this. "As if we were separated in some other life and needed to find each other before we could understand again what happiness is…." He trailed off, thinking she would find this utterly insane.

Allison did not move her hands away from Jess's. Tears began to run down her cheeks. She kept holding one of his hands as she used a napkin to blot her face. "I feel the same way. I've always been sensible and logical, but when we met the other night, my whole world was turned upside down. I just knew that I had to see you again. It felt like a part of me had been missing and was suddenly being miraculously returned."

The waitress appeared, and they asked for another minute before ordering. They smiled at each other like old friends and picked up the menus. The meal was adequate, but the time passed at warp speed in a blur of sensations. They vaguely remembered enjoying soup and a vegetable and noodle dish. But what remained forever in their minds was the strong attraction they felt that seemed, if possible, to intensify with each moment they were together.

Where to go to sit and talk was the next hurdle. David, the landlady's son, was home from school for the holidays, so the house in Potomac was not an option. Allison shared a townhouse with three other women. There was no question in Jess's mind that they would continue their conversation that night. He sensed that Allison shared his conclusion. Jess put his thoughts into words, hoping that he was doing the right thing. "We have two choices: to walk in frigid weather in the parks all night or to rent a hotel room where we can have comfort and privacy."

The hotel room was the obvious choice. Without further discussion, they somehow reached complete agreement. They dropped off Allison's car at her apartment and sitting in comfortable silence, Jess drove in the direction of Bethesda. They found a room at the Doubletree Hotel. Once in the room, Jess and Allison shrugged out of their winter coats and sank into the two comfortable chairs facing each other across from the two queen sized beds. What followed was a torrent of words that tumbled out of each in turn.

Allison spoke about growing up in a suburb of Boston and of her father, Bill, an MIT graduate who was currently working with NASA on an offshoot of the Daedalus Project. Her mother, Sylvia, taught kindergarten in the public school. Allison had no siblings.

Allison had graduated from Mount Holyoke in 1982. She had gone on to take courses and the qualifying exam to be a CPA. She celebrated her 22nd birthday by starting a job in the District as an accountant at one of the many national companies that use Wisconsin Avenue as their address. The company acted as a clearing house for every award trophy and recognition prize imaginable. Now, at age 23, it provided an excellent income and benefits and as a 9-5 job with no "homework" left Allison free to pursue her hobby, which was computer programming.

Her parents had moved recently to Manassas, Virginia to be near her father's project which was based at the Manassas airfield. Allison was thrilled, as she was very close to her parents and enjoyed visiting them. She shared a townhouse in Chevy Chase with several other women who each went their separate ways but collaborated on rent and utilities.

Both Allison and Jess had dated sporadically and enjoyed the company of others, but had never found anyone who was of great interest to them as a life partner. Jess told of his college background and his job in the Maryland suburbs. He had grown up in the small town of Waterloo, New York, in the Finger Lakes region, and his father had worked as a station master on the Lehigh Valley Railroad. The income from his father's job was sufficient for their financial needs, and his mother had not worked outside the home. His parents had wanted a large family, but this did not happen. He was their only child. His Dad took his railroad retirement as soon as he qualified, and they moved to a small condo in Sarasota, Florida.

Now, at age 28, Jess was established in his computer programming job and the teaching opportunity at Montgomery College, but he confided to Allison that he was ready for the chance to live a fuller, more interesting and more professionally challenging life.

That night, at the Doubletree, they talked on about their hopes and dreams, and sometime toward dawn they found they were exhausted (each in a strangely pleasant way) and they each lay down on one of the beds and fell into a deep sleep.

Jess woke first. As his eyes slowly opened, he wondered at first where he was. Then, looking over at the other bed, what had seemed like a wonderful dream flooded back into his mind. He sat up, yawned, raked his fingers through his rumpled hair and stood for a minute next to the other bed looking down at the woman who had totally transformed his life in just a few short days. Allison's beautiful 5-foot-9-inch body stretched out under the blanket, her shining crown of black curls spread on the pillow. Her skin was a very light bronze in color, her lips were formed in the suggestion of a smile, her eye lashes were long and even in sleep there was a luminosity that, to him, seemed to make her glow softly. Just looking at her filled him with undulating waves of love and joy. He bent quietly and brushed a kiss just above her lips.

In the movies, this might have been the time when the male lead would have dressed rapidly, left a note with money and cab fare and slinked away rather than take a chance on the commitment that was sure to come. Jess had no such thoughts. He couldn't wait to spend the rest of his life as the friend, husband, and soul mate of this amazing woman. "Bring it on!" he silently shouted to whatever entity was in charge of the Universe.

Then he turned and went into the bathroom to use the hotel toiletry kit to shower, shave, brush his teeth and try to make himself as presentable as possible.

Allison woke and stretched luxuriously in the comfortable bed. She was used to waking to the growing chorus of voices as her housemates bustled around preparing for the morning commute to work. Today it was quiet, except for … she looked over at the other bed. Jess was not in it, but she could hear the shower. She smiled and felt the pleasure that his proximity brought to her. She was connected to him somehow in a way she had never felt with anyone else. It was mysterious, and at the same time it was the most exciting, most fulfilling sensation she had ever known. It did not have the feel of some superficial romantic love affair. She knew what that was. She had briefly thought she was in love with a brilliant student in her freshman year in college. They had met at a party after a football game at Yale. The glow lasted only a few weeks, and then reality hit. She was physically attracted to the young man, but they had little in common except for high grades in school. He was heading for a career in diplomatic circles and made no secret of the fact that he was, as a junior at Yale, already looking for a possible candidate as a wife who would enhance his future position.

There was no comparison, no frame of reference marvelous enough to describe her feelings toward Jess. This was a total mystery to her. The attraction was so strong, so completely right. She wiggled her toes and shivered with pleasure at the thought of him. She propped herself up on the pillows and waited for her turn to shower and dress for the day. When Jess emerged from the bathroom already dressed, she slipped past him with a smile and soon joined him drying her unruly curls with a towel.

They looked at each other and then stood in the center of the room and exchanged a long, delicious kiss. They held each other wordlessly for a long minute. "What shall we do next" Jess asked in a husky voice as he looked into those deep hazel pools that were Allison's eyes. How he loved her. Whatever she wanted he would gladly move heaven and earth to make it happen. She couldn't speak at first, the emotion was so strong. Finally, she said, "Let's go and change our clothes and then drive to Manassas so that you can meet my parents."

His heart sang at those words. "My thoughts exactly," he said with a smile.

They had a quick breakfast in the hotel dining room, paid the bill, and warmed up the car. It was a very cold December Saturday, and the defroster worked overtime to keep the windshield clear. They went to Potomac first, picked up Jess's things, and then went on to the townhouse in Chevy Chase. They had left Allison's car there the night before, and they decided to continue to Manassas in Jess's 1980 Dodge Diplomat.

Allison invited Jess in to meet everyone, but her housemates had all left for the day. She telephoned her parents, who were at home and delighted at the prospect of a visit. Her mother insisted that they plan to be there at 1:00 for lunch.

Back in the car, they talked non-stop as they headed south into Fairfax and then Prince William County in Virginia. Allison pointed out a number of areas where farm land was sprouting new home communities. "There is such a demand right now for housing in the suburbs," she told him. "Some of these communities feature really extraordinary houses." He smiled. "Would you like to live in one?"

"I wasn't thinking of that," she replied. "I was thinking that right here, right now there are unlimited opportunities for an architect."

"You've uncovered my secret passion," he said with a slow smile. "Architecture is my hobby, but I've been thinking that it's time to consider making it my career. What would you think of being married to a struggling young architect?"

Allison grinned, "Would it be helpful if your wife was an accountant who could keep all the funds in balance?"

By the time they reached Manassas they were in a spirited discussion of what the steps forward would be both for Jess's new career and for their wedding and living arrangements. Jess stopped the car and pulled into an empty church parking lot a few blocks from their destination. They kissed and held each other for a long moment. Jess broke the silence. "I think we're agreed that I am about to meet your parents and to ask them for the hand of their daughter in marriage. We should probably agree on when the wedding will be and a few other details."

Allison smiled her beaming smile. "What do you think about an April wedding? I know that's the sensible compromise between today and the traditional June date, but I would have preferred maybe next Tuesday or Wednesday!"

"We can start looking for an apartment and if we plan the wedding for April 2nd, we'll be moving in at the beginning of a month. We can be engaged sometime between today and next Wednesday!"

Jess put his arms around her and they kissed again. Neither wanted to stop, but it was getting close to one o'clock. They left the car parked in the church parking lot and walked toward their destination, snuggling together. Allison pointed to a modest colonial house a short way down the picture perfect residential street. There was a wreath of pine boughs on the eight-panel front door. The yard was covered with snow, which served to accent the neat hedge and the stately evergreens. Allison burst through the front door, pulling Jess along after her. "Mom, Dad, come and meet your future son-in-law!" They were ecstatic. Everyone spoke at once, and suddenly Mr. and Mrs. Myers stopped talking and stood back and looked at Jess for a moment. Then, Bill Myers said, "Let's sit down and get acquainted, Son." Sylvia Myers smiled and took Jess's hand. "I think we can get acquainted while we eat lunch."

They followed her to the dining room which was just as cheerful and inviting as the entry hall had been. The table was set with simple elegance, and the food smelled delicious. There was homemade lasagna and freshly baked bread. The salad was filled with fresh vegetables. Jess was suddenly very hungry. Compliments abounded for the cook. Allison and her mother cleared the table and brought in coffee and pieces of freshly baked apple pie.

Bill and Jess talked about their educational backgrounds and interests. The unmanned space flights in which Bill was involved at NASA were of great interest to Jess. Bill told him that he had never doubted for a moment what he wanted to work at once he came in contact with the group at MIT that was working on the Daedalus project. Jess intimated to Bill that his attraction to architecture was nudging him into considering that field full time. "You're in the right place for that!" Bill assured him. "There is such a need for architects here right now. Will you set up your own office or work in an established firm?"

Jess had thought this through and answered, "I have enough savings and enough contacts in the area to go on my own. I want to be my own boss. Between now and April I hope to continue with my computer programming job and at the same time open an architectural office in northern Virginia and start making bids on plans for upscale homes."

"What happens in April?" Sylvia asked.

"That is when, with the blessing of her parents, Allison and I hope to marry."

There was the briefest moment of silence, and then Bill raised his water glass. "A toast to the bride and groom!" he said enthusiastically. They all raised their glasses. Everyone helped to clear the table and Allison loaded the dishwasher. Within 15 minutes, Allison and her mother were sitting in the living room animatedly discussing wedding plans.

Jess followed Bill to the third bay of the garage, which was set up as a spacious and cozy office. A display case held models of prototypes of the Daedalus and other human-powered planes. Bill took a few of them out one by one and handed each to Jess in turn, explaining as he did so the history and developmental process involved in each. Jess was captivated by these experimental aircraft and the concept that led from them to some of the present advances in unmanned flights into space. They also discussed the NASA programs of weather-related scientific studies. The time flew by. Eventually, Allison and Sylvia joined them, and after hugs and invitations to return as soon as possible, Allison and Jess left for Maryland.

Snuggling up against Jess in the spacious bench front seat of the Dodge, and inhaling the wonderful scent of his leather jacket, Allison smiled and sighed contentedly. "I'll call my folks as soon as I get to my room," Jess said. "They will be so happy!" "Ummm," Alison replied. That was her last utterance until they reached Chevy Chase. They were both lost in their thoughts and the wonder of all that was happening.

"I'll call you as soon as I talk to my parents," Jess told her as they kissed and hugged on the snowy sidewalk outside the townhouse. "I love you, Allison."

"And I love you so very much," she whispered.

Chapter Four
The Plans

Jess dialed the phone and heard his Dad answer almost immediately. As the ring signal began, he could picture Wade Sampson with his gray crewcut, lively gray eyes and black framed glasses and his ever-present wide grin showing the crinkles of laugh lines on either side of his mouth. He would be wearing a colorful Hawaiian shirt and trim fitting navy shorts with white socks and sneakers. Wade worked out every day and his lean, muscular, 6-foot body and his friendly face made a handsome combination. Wade loved his wife deeply, and his love and respect were reciprocated. His Mom, Mary Sampson, was of medium height. Her slim brown legs and trim figure gave her the look of a fashion model no matter what she wore. She would have a blue and white checked apron over her shorts and shirt and would be just about to serve supper.

"Hello," Wade's deep voice came over the phone.

"Hi Dad."

"Oh, Jess, hello, son! Mary, it's our boy!"

Jess could hear his mother calling from the kitchen. At the sound of the name of the caller, he could hear her running excitedly toward the telephone table. He could picture her blue eyes sparkling, her curls bouncing. Then they were both there sharing the receiver.

"Hello, you two. I have some news."

Mary sounded concerned. "Is everything all right? You haven't had an accident in all that snow, have you?"

"No, Mom, I've never been better! I'm calling with GOOD news! The best! Are you ready? I am engaged, and Allison and I will be married in April!"

Both parents answered together with great excitement,

Wade: "I'm so happy to hear that, son. Allison, eh? What…."

Mary interrupted, "Oh, Jess, how wonderful! Have you planned the wedding? I'll have to get busy if you want us to think of people to invite. Where will the wedding be? Can you send us a picture…?"

Jess laughed and assured them both that a photo would be in the mail as soon as possible (he said to himself that he should have thought of that). He told them that it would be a small church wedding; that he would welcome their suggestions for guests, that it would be in Virginia in or near Manassas, and that he would call them with the exact date as soon as Allison and her parents (who were, by the way, wonderful people) had arranged it.

The call ended with hearty congratulations from his father and tears of happiness from his mother. He could picture them sitting down to a macaroni-and-cheese casserole or beef goulash and talking it all over. He smiled and dialed Allison's number. He was alone in the house that night, so he would be able to speak freely with her. He gave her the good news and listened as she told him about the call from her mother, who was going over a to-do list of things she would tackle on Monday regarding reservations for the church, the organist, the location of the reception, invitations, photographer, etc.

"Oh, speaking of photographers," he interjected, "my parents would like to see a picture of you. Come to think of it, I'd love to have one to carry in my wallet. Can we find a local photography studio where we can have some taken?"

"Yes. I'll look into it on Monday. Mom mentioned that she would like us to have one taken together for the engagement announcement. It is exciting, but a bit overwhelming, too, to have all these rituals converging on us at once!"

"I know what you mean, but I've already decided that it's worth all of the inconveniences that are sure to roll in! The reward for enduring it is a lifetime with you!"

"I agree totally," she said, and he could feel the warmth of her smile.

"Will I see you tomorrow?"

"Of course! Do you want to meet at the computer lab? It should be fairly quiet there on a Sunday."

"Good idea! Is 1:00 good for you?"

"Perfect. See you then. I love you!"

"I love you, Allison. Tomorrow seems so far away…"

After they hung up, Jess showered and went to bed without doing any of the reading he had planned. He was exhausted and happy in a way he had never experienced before. As he drifted off to sleep he was sure he could feel Allison's presence as if she had touched his soul and was expanding his field of vision. It was a marvelous phenomenon, but sleep overtook him before he could analyze it. He just knew that he and she were somehow miraculously entwined forever in a way he could not intellectually understand.

Meanwhile, Bill and Sylvia Myers made gentle yet passionate love to each other. Afterward, floating toward sleep, Bill asked, "Do you think that Jess and Allison are making love with each other tonight?"

"Knowing Allison and meeting Jess just today, I will have to say that I don't think so. I think Jess is a man who will ask Allison what she wants to do about that, even though the desire will be equally strong for both. She will probably say she prefers for now to wait, but that they can reevaluate along the way at any time. That's my guess."

"I wonder how long they've known each other," Bill mused.

"That's a question we wouldn't ask, and it didn't come up. I'm grateful that we've always trusted Allison's judgment. I think she was born with the sound judgment of a mature adult!"

"Yes, we really got lucky! Whether they met a year ago or last week isn't significant. They are definitely perfectly matched from what I saw today!"

Sylvia kissed her husband and curled up next to him, sharing his love. They slept soundly and dreamed with great anticipation of what was to come.

On Sunday, Jess had a chance to see his landlady and he told her of his coming marriage. He also took the bold step of giving her notice that he would be terminating his month-to-month arrangement with her on the last day of February. This would give her a chance to find a new tenant for the room. She was a bit disappointed to lose such a trouble-free tenant, but she thanked him for the timely notice and wished him well.

He stopped at the gym to exercise, and by 12:30 he was at the lab. He felt Allison's presence before he heard the door handle turn. There she was, dressed in her navy blue coat with a colorful scarf around her neck and those amazing black curls cascading down her back. They were alone in the lab, and he walked slowly over to her and took her in his arms. "I have to ask you something right now while it is in the front of my mind," he whispered. "When do you want me to make love to you? I want to so much, but I need to know what you want to do…."

Allison stayed in the embrace as she answered huskily, "I want to so much too! Right this minute there is nothing I want more! But there is a part of me that wants to wait until or at least close to the wedding. I want the love-making to be so essential to our relationship that it is connected with the ceremony in which we pledge to love and give ourselves to each other in every way for the rest of our lives. Does that make sense?"

He pulled her closer and smiled as he said, "Perfect sense, darling. I know our love-making will be spectacular whenever it happens, but I agree that it will be even more valuable if it comes along with our marriage promises at the wedding."

They kissed and wanted to stand that way until the wedding, but there was someone coming down the corridor, so they moved over to sit at a couple of computers. They sat, but they didn't make a move to power on the machines. They just looked at each other with love.

"Let's go to the mall and look at engagement rings," Jess said.

"What an impulsive lover," Allison teased. "OK, let's go!"

Chapter Five
Love and Marriage, 1987

The days and weeks rushed by in a blur of activity. Allison and Jess settled into a familiar routine. On Saturdays, they would go to Manassas and spend the afternoon with Sylvia and Bill. On Sundays, they went to the computer lab and worked on whatever innovations and advances had appeared that week. Jess spent Saturday mornings at his drafting table adding to his design portfolio and by early February was ready to set up appointments with some of the builders in the area. He had moved into the District and now lived in a spacious, upscale apartment on Rhode Island Avenue. The rent had been at a bargain rate, as he had been willing to sign a one-year lease in the middle of winter. This would be their first home after the wedding. There was a large modern living room with wide windows that looked out on the surrounding area, a well-equipped kitchen, a small dining room, two bedrooms (one of which was Jess's office) and two full baths.

He and Allison had liked the apartment from the moment they saw it. The rent was within their budget, and the address would be advantageous to Jess's architectural business as well as being an easy commute to Allison's office. There was even a heated underground garage.

On the first Saturday after Jess moved in, they entertained Allison's parents there. RSVPs were rapidly coming in to the invitations that Allison and Sylvia had sent out. They estimated that there would be 150 guests at the wedding in All Saints Episcopal Church in Dale City where Allison's parents attended services more or less regularly. They knew the rector, and everything had been easy to arrange. The church was modest in size and had a warm and friendly ambience. Allison had not been a regular church goer since her confirmation at age 12, but both Jess and Allison agreed to attend the four-mandatory marriage-preparation classes. They decided that the classes were useful, as the curriculum was designed to emphasize the importance of couples working together in areas such as finances and family planning. What were the views of the persons planning marriage as to who would keep track of expenses, where income would be deposited, who would have access to what funds, etc.? In the area of family planning, did both partners want children, if so, when and how many? How would holidays be spent? How would major holidays be celebrated – with his relatives or hers? What about social life? Would either partner be free to spend leisure time outside of the home whenever they chose? Marriages often failed when these issues were not addressed before the wedding. Ample time was allotted during the classes for private, honest discussions.

Jess and Allison both came from homes where positive values and respectful, loving behaviors had been modeled for them. They found they were in agreement on these points. Their checking, savings, and investment accounts would all be joint with each having access to all. Allison would keep track of income and expenses and prepare income tax returns. They hoped to have children as soon as possible. They could afford it and could also afford to have Allison work from home as a part-time CPA when the time came. She would give up her corporate job at that time.

Socially, they would attend work-related functions together. They would work out together and spend time together with friends. Neither was interested in going out without the other. They didn't drink or "hang out." They both enjoyed jazz and classical music and looked forward to attending musical performances together or with another couple and discussing it afterward. They also pictured themselves reading books and articles and discussing them in their leisure time. "Is this how old married couples are described?" Allison asked. "Sure is!" Jess answered and kissed her right there in the room at the church where they were discussing the serious side of marriage.

They also agreed that holiday gatherings would be discussed by all family members as they arose. Both sets of parents were becoming acquainted by telephone, and it was fun to look forward to meeting them in person in a few weeks. Once the marriage preparation course was over, they turned their full attention to Jess's presentations of his portfolio. He had received encouraging messages from Pulte Builders and, more notably, from a firm that was receiving contracts to build custom homes. He followed up with both and was given the opportunity to look at a plat plan in a subdivision called Forest Glen near Falls Church. The lots were all wooded and the smallest was five acres. The development bordered a wildlife preserve with a lovely stream and a scenic view from every direction. Allison and Jess spent a Sunday looking over the plat plan, walking the lots, and imagining what would look best on each of the distinctive pieces of land. Jess made sketches on site and within ten days had drawn up plans for the elevations of each of the 12 homes that were slated to be built there.

A week later, he was invited to meet with the CEO and the company president in Arlington, Virginia. In a detailed discussion, they gave Jess the commission to design the homes to specifications developed with the prospective purchasers of each home site. Allison and Jess were ecstatic. This would be a full-time job with the prospect of much more to come. They decided that Jess would give notice at his computer programming job immediately, effective in two weeks and that he would continue with the part-time teaching until the end of the semester. This was the break they had hoped for. It was coming at an accelerated pace because of the explosion of new homes in the northern Virginia suburbs. Salaries in Washington were rising, commuters abounded, and the government workers at all levels wanted distinctive, custom-built homes in the suburbs.

At about the same time, Sylvia and Bill surprised them by talking with them in detail about the wedding gift they had decided to give them. After Saturday dinner, they went into the living room for coffee as usual, and Bill brought in a map and a plat plan. "This is an investment we made a few years ago when the real-estate market was on the verge of heating up," he said. "I think you may want to consider it as a home site for a starter home for you and your family. We bought four lots. We built a spec house on the one that is a double, wooded lot. The other two are near the lake, and will sell with or without a house on them. The lots are still in demand. Most of the subdivision has been developed, and it is considered a desirable location for families with jobs in the district or for those who are stationed at Quantico. The schools are excellent, and it is not very far from Manassas. Sylvia and I want to give you all four lots as a wedding gift. No strings attached! We will be delighted with any and all of your choices as to what to do with them." Bill pointed out the location of the lots as Allison and Jess thanked them profusely.

After dinner, they all drove to the location in Montclair for a guided tour of their wedding gift. The double lot with the house already on it was perfect! It was at the curved center of a tree-lined cul de sac. The design was colonial and the siding was red brick. There was a good sized front yard, a two-car garage, and a level driveway. The wooded lot sloped down gracefully in back. The finished, walk-out basement opened onto a beautiful lawn that, Allison noted, had the perfect place for a sandbox and a swing set. Looking up, they could imagine the patio they would build off the living room.

Inside, they found a modern eat-in kitchen, a formal dining room, living room, a half bath and a family room on the first floor. Upstairs were four bedrooms, two full baths, and a laundry room. There was lots of closet and storage space and a full attic. They concluded that this was much more than a starter house. This was a home that would endure from wedding to retirement.

"Did you ever try to sell the house, Dad?" Allison asked.

"No. We thought about it at first, but we both came to the conclusion that this was the house for our daughter, our son-in-law, and our grandchildren. Life presents enough challenges, and we wanted to ease the burden in this one area. We kept it a surprise, and had fun coming over and mowing the lawn and dusting once in a while. You don't mind that we didn't tell you until now, do you, Allison?"

Allison hugged her parents and told them that she certainly didn't mind the secret and that they were the best parents on the planet. They drove through Montclair and looked at the golf course and the lake. Jess immediately imagined just the right house to be built for the buyers of the lake lots. He was overwhelmed with happiness and with gratitude. They went back to the house on the cul de sac. While Sylvia and Allison talked about drapes and color choices, he and Bill examined the area where the patio would be constructed and discussed everything from concrete footers to lumber and dimensions.

They were all totally at ease with each other and had already become family. The wedding was a joint project that flowed smoothly and effortlessly, with Sylvia's guidance. They decided that they would keep the Latrobe apartment as Jess's Washington DC office for the remainder of the lease but would move their living quarters to Montclair right after the wedding.

Chapter Six

To Have and to Hold from
This Time Forward

Allison, Jess, and all of the guests pronounced the wedding to be perfect. Allison and Jess loved the house, and they both felt as if they were floating on a perpetual cloud of joy.

They had stood before the minister in the little church and pledged their love and their lives to each other. They had been immediately surrounded by parents and friends as they walked from the altar out into the bright spring day. Allison remembered it afterward as a sweet symphony in which she and Jess were joined together in a bond of pure love that could not be severed in life or in death. They spent their first week together in their new home and could not have chosen a better place for a wedding trip.

They played music on the hi-fi and danced. They cooked meals together. They made love passionately at all hours of the day and night. They talked for hours at a time and never tired of each other's company. It was a dream that became reality. There was a bond between them that was more than a contract or even a covenant. It was a coming together and entwining of their spirits so that they truly became two separate individuals who were at the same time, one in spirit.

Allison began to work as a CPA from an office in nearby Dumfries and Jess from his home office. He still made trips into Washington, DC to attend meetings, and he still did some work from the apartment there. But more and more, as his work became known and his client list grew, he was able to work from the office in their home. When the apartment lease in the District was up, he rented some office space near

Montclair for client meetings. Jess and Allison were at the right place at the right time, just as Allison had predicted. The demand for custom-built homes was growing by the day. Jess could be as busy as he wanted to be.

Jess and the second man he now also called "Dad" set to work designing and building a patio off the living room with wide, safe steps down into the backyard where the sandbox and swing set would be installed. They all met, as before, on Saturdays and alternated between the house in Manassas and the one in Montclair.

Chapter Seven
Gail Louise Sampson, 1988

They realized, with great joy, about three weeks after the wedding that Allison was pregnant. This was confirmed by a visit to the obstetrician, Virginia Stedman, MD, and the news was presented to both sets of parents in mid-May. There was much joy and excitement all around, and Allison glowed with good health and happiness. Jess and Allison had selected the midwife who would help them to deliver the baby at home. Her name was Janet Wells and she had been a hospital delivery-room nurse before she had decided in 1984 to enroll in the master's degree program at the Georgetown University School of Nursing and to seek accreditation through that program as a midwife. Since graduation, she had delivered many babies and had glowing recommendations.

Janet met with Jess and Allison once a week starting in July to go over the exercises that would prepare Allison for the delivery. They became good friends over the months, and invited Janet to move into their guest bedroom right after the first of the year so that she would be on hand when Allison's labor began.

Janet was available starting on January 5 and they anticipated that the baby would be born around the 14th. As it turned out, they didn't have to wait that long. Janet moved into the guest room on the 5th. It was such a pleasant experience. Janet was a woman of average height with a slender figure and a round, smiling face with deep brown eyes. She wore her abundant waves of auburn hair loose and it cascaded around her shoulders and down her back. She had a quick wit and a great sense of humor. They all laughed together every time they sat down for a meal because Jess and Janet would start telling stories of what had happened with their clients. Jess told about a woman who made plans to have him design a custom house for her and her two sons. He asked her income and she reported that it was $200,000. This meant that she was in the income bracket to be considered for a mortgage on a new home if her finances were in good shape.

She sat down with his assistant to give her financial qualifications. He soon came into Jess and asked for help. The woman had an annual income of $200,000 per year. She also had 23 credit cards with an average balance on each of $1200. And a car loan on her Mercedes of $50,000. Her total investment and savings were $0! She was shocked that she did not qualify!

He also told about the couple who were well qualified with high income, a healthy investment portfolio, and many thousands in savings from which they would pay cash. The drawback was that for the $400,000 price of the house they wanted it to be totally customized to their specifications. The price was commensurate with that of a beautiful and spacious home that would be built within certain specifications. The couple wanted, for the basic price, custom shelves throughout, crown molding, a swimming pool and many, many other amenities. They threatened to publicly expose Jess's company as a fraud if these items were not included in the contract. Jess's lawyer discovered that the couple had blackmailed three other builders in this way. The couple immediately backed down.

Janet told about a family who were expecting their second child. They lived in a small condo in Vienna, VA. They had set aside a space in their small home for the baby's room. They also had a small car, but planned to all squeeze together and live within their income. The plan was for the wife to stay home with the children. The husband was making a moderate income, but it was hoped it would increase over time and she could remain at home.

A pre-natal exam revealed that instead of one baby, there were possibly two. When the wife went into labor, Janet discovered that there were indeed two babies, identical twin girls. The husband and wife were in a state of shock in spite of the prediction. As Janet prepared to deliver the afterbirth, something totally unexpected happened! A third baby girl appeared in the birth canal. This sent the parents into something like the aftermath of an earthquake. Janet telephoned a doctor who had been standing by, and he came to the condo. Together, they completed the delivery, weighed and measured the babies, and snuggle them into the crib that had been intended and prepared for one infant.

The babies were close to full term and all were healthy and at least 4 pounds each. Clothing had to be purchased that day, as there were not enough sleepers and diapers for this crowd. Janet said that the mother sat up in her bed shaking her head and looking stunned, saying, "I have to go to work. I have to go to work!" Their little boy thought it was all great fun. Fortunately, their friends and neighbors and work associates pitched in and not only gave donations of clothing, etc. but took shifts coming to the condo and helping with the care and feeding of the babies for several months. The mother's boss, a lawyer, arranged for her to work from home. An auto dealership gained much favorable publicity by presenting the family with a Honda Pilot automobile.

Allison and Jess loved that story, but they both declared they hoped to produce their children in single digits ... one at a time. Janet assured them that she saw no similarity in Allison's case to that of the mother of the triplets.

All went so smoothly that they were almost surprised when labor began on January 10. Janet's and Allison's calmness reassured Jess, who was confident in Janet's skill but concerned for his beloved wife at the same time. Jess and Allison worked together as they had been instructed. The hours went by and as the contractions grew stronger, Allison found relief in standing and then kneeling in the warm shower. When it was time to push, Janet was calm and kind and in perfect harmony with the work Allison was doing to bring their baby into the world. Suddenly there was the strong, miraculous sound of their daughter's cry and there she was.

Jess telephoned Sylvia and Bill and Wade and Mary with the good news. The baby nursed eagerly, held tenderly in Allison's arms. Allison was laughing and crying at the same time. Then it was Jess's turn to hold his tiny daughter, and he felt tears come to his eyes. She was a little wrinkled, but he could see she would be a replica of Allison. She had tufts of rather unruly black hair, clear hazel eyes, and dimples on each side of her tiny mouth. He was sure she smiled at him as they looked into each other's eyes. Allison and he concluded that their daughter, Gail Louise Sampson, was absolutely extraordinary, but they agreed to keep this to themselves and not brag. Each set of grandparents, of course, came to the same conclusion independently.

Janet promised to return to be with the parents who were now her close friends, when the next addition to the family was due to arrive.

Chapter Eight
Sarah Ellen Sampson, 1991

They decided to try for a companion to little Gail before their daughter reached the age where she might be so used to being the only child that she could have second thoughts about the introduction of a sibling. And so it was that their second daughter, Sarah Ellen Sampson, arrived in April of 1991 just after their fourth wedding anniversary and Gail's third birthday.

Janet Wells remarked that Sarah could easily be mistaken for Gail's twin if their baby pictures were placed side by side. From birth, Sarah looked like an exact replica of her beautiful, spirited sister. They were so similar in looks and gestures that it was uncanny. Jess loved them and Allison and his life so much that he sometimes wondered if it was all a phenomenal dream. By the time Sarah arrived, Allison had given up the office in Dumfries and was thrilled to stay at home with the girls. She was living the life she had always dreamed would be hers, and so was Jess.

By the time Gail started kindergarten, there was a new pre-school program in place in the local school system. They decided not to enroll Sarah in it. They agreed that age five was soon enough to begin school. Sarah was already able to read, and Allison made sure both girls had friends to play with in the neighborhood and spent lots of time walking outdoors and exploring the trails and natural beauty that surrounded them in Montclair. They also loved walking around the lake and playing at the park.

Gail was an excellent student and enthusiastically involved in any activity she tackled. Her love of learning was shared by her sister, as Gail sat Sarah down on a regular basis and taught her whatever Gail had learned in school. Sarah was a willing student, and she started kindergarten the following year with a solid foundation in reading, arithmetic, and science.

They all had fun together as a family. That was their main goal.

Chapter Nine
Devastation and Transition, 1995

It was raining and thundering when they woke on that morning in late March, and for a few minutes Jess and Allison discussed the possibility that the field trip would be cancelled. Jess recalled the delicious love making of the night before, and reached out to pull Allison into his arms, kissing her and whispering into her ear, "I love you, you beautiful woman!" Allison kissed him passionately and then ruffled his hair. (He loved it when she did that). "Not now," she said. "I have to get the girls up and ready for this field trip. If it's called off because of rain, I'll be back. So, just give me a raincheck!" They laughed, kissed again, climbed out of bed and began the morning routine.

A phone call verified that the school trip to the Smithsonian was still on, and by 9:00 a.m. Allison and the girls had kissed and hugged Jess, were safely buckled into the Subaru and on their way. He puttered around the office for about an hour and then headed toward Falls Church for a meeting with Summit Builders.

Jess and his associate, Jack, spent the morning going over plans for the new project, went to lunch around 1:00 and then met with the sales team for about an hour. During the meeting, as one of the sales people was giving a progress report, Jess distinctly heard Allison speak to him. Her sweet, loving voice had an urgency about it that he had not heard before. The message was brief but insistent. He clearly heard Allison say to him, "Don't worry, Darling, Sarah, Gail, and I are all right. We are fine, and we love you."

At 3:30 Jess's beeper went off, and he returned the call. He was standing beside Jack's desk listening to the voice on the other end of the line when he turned pale and sank into a chair in front of the desk and his head slumped into his free hand. Jack ran around the desk and sat beside him. Jess handed Jack the phone and putting his head in both hands, began to sob uncontrollably. Emma, Jack's assistant ran over and knelt in front of Jess. She tilted back her head and looked up at him with her kind eyes. "What is it, Jess? Is it Allison?"

Jess couldn't speak. He couldn't stop sobbing. Jack hung up the phone and put his arm around the shoulders of his friend. "I'll call Bill," he said softly.

Everything that happened from there was a slowly moving blur to Jess. Bill arrived and brought with him the family doctor. The doctor gave Jess an injection and a prescription. Bill drove Jess and the doctor to Manassas and after dropping the doctor back at his office, took Jess to their house where Sylvia was waiting for them. Jess could see that she had been crying. They all sat silently in the living room for a while. Then Sylvia took his hand and said to Jess, "Will you stay here with us for a while, son?" Bill's voice was hoarse when he added encouragement to this idea.

Jess was still not in a state of mind to accept that his wife and children were gone. "Killed instantly," the trooper had told him on the phone. "A terrible accident caused by a tractor-trailer truck going out of control, skidding, crossing the median and crushing the Subaru beyond recognition." He couldn't think of it or try to picture it. He could only hold onto Allison's message to him which had come to him at what he now knew was the time of the crash. "Don't worry, Darling, Sarah, Gail, and I are all right. We are fine, and we love you."

He told Sylvia and Bill what he had heard. He explained the timing of it. This telling seemed, oddly, to comfort him. It also caused a change in Sylvia. She looked at Bill with what Jess could only call a knowing glance and they both considered the words for several minutes. Then Sylvia explained. "Jess, soon after we married, I was told by our gynecologist that we could not have children.

"We accepted that. As much as we had wanted a family, we decided that if it was not meant to be we would just somehow get along as we were. We love each other very much and we are so happy being together. Well, ten years went by, and suddenly for no logical reason, I discovered I was pregnant. We were thrilled and made all the preparations that we had thought we could never experience. Allison arrived in the middle of a snow storm and we barely made it to the hospital. She was a most unusual child. Now, I know that all parents usually believe that of their children, but she had a grace and maturity about her that is just not common.

"We loved her to distraction. She was never a challenge in the area of discipline. She just seemed to know intuitively how to entertain herself and how to make us happy. She was polite and kind to other children, but she seemed to be of another world and did not form deep relationships with them. She had imaginary friends that she said taught her things like geography and math and science.

"She could read when she was three years old. Her vocabulary was advanced before she went to school. She was tolerant of school, but she could complete any assignment on her own, and received an A in almost all of them. She had a great love of nature and delighted in knowing the names of birds, plants, and trees. In short, it was as if we had been sent an angel daughter.

"Jess, you are our son now, and we love you. I have a feeling that you will hear more from our Allison. She chose you as her life partner, and she loved and cherished you. She is reaching out to you now to let you know that she and the girls are really fine. They are in a wonderful place that we can only imagine. They will be with us always, and they will reach out to us again. I'm convinced of it! "

By then, the sun had gone down and night had arrived with a cloudless sky and millions of stars. The moon shone brightly. Jess wanted to go home, but he dreaded being there alone. He would stay here with his second parents. They would go to the house in the morning, and together they would face all of the work that had to be done. Life would never be the same for him. Tears leapt to his eyes as he tried to reach out and feel Allison's presence. He was very quiet as he looked out at the clear night that had followed the morning's torrential rain. Sylvia was in the kitchen preparing a light supper. No one was hungry, but they would eat enough to stay healthy and to have the energy for what lay ahead. He closed his eyes and felt a sensation that he knew well.

It was the feeling he had always had when Allison was coming into the room. It was a combination of excitement and the anticipation of her approaching him. He remained still, just letting the feeling wash over him. He could almost feel her now. She was on his left, and she was putting her arms around him. He moved into the feeling and they rested together in a loving embrace. He said softly, in a voice that was a low whisper, "Allison, I love you so much." He felt rather than heard her answer. He felt the radiance of the smile, the smile that belonged to no one but Allison. He leaned into her for a wonderful moment. Then she was gone, but some of the energy that had surrounded her remained with him.

He joined Sylvia and Bill in the kitchen. They nibbled at grilled cheese sandwiches and drank chamomile tea. After that, they made a plan to go to the house in Montclair at 8:00 the next morning, and finally they went off to sleep as much as possible on this, the saddest day of their lives.

Chapter Ten
Family Ties in Two Worlds, 1995

Jess was thrilled when his parents came to visit for two weeks in late May. It was the first he had seen them since the blur of their two day visit for the funeral in March. He met them at Dulles Airport and enjoyed their enthusiasm at seeing some of the nearby areas of Fairfax County where he had been the architect for some outstanding designer homes. They wanted to see more right away. All suggestions of going home to rest were immediately vetoed. It was a brilliant sunny day and they especially wanted to see the new development he had described to them on the telephone. He gladly took them on a tour and found they were as enthusiastic about the property as he was. He had the recently approved plat plan in the SUV. He pulled it out, and they insisted on driving along the trail and then walking each of the five-acre lots. The colonial two-story style of home was the most desired by buyers in that market, and Jess had made sketches with that in mind. His parents were enthusiastic about the proposed designs and thought that everything would be sold in record time.

They stopped for dinner and talked non-stop during and after the meal. Once they reached the house, everyone was suddenly quiet. "How is it for you, Jess … coming home to this house every day…?"

"Sometimes it's hard, Mom," he answered, "and sometimes it's REALLY hard," he added, turning away so she wouldn't see the tears in his eyes. "But I wouldn't want to live anywhere else! All of our memories are here. I definitely feel the presence of Allison and our daughters. They keep me encouraged."

Wade put his hand gently on Jess's, but he couldn't speak. They stood looking at the house that had been the place in which their much-loved son and daughter-in-law had lived so happily after their marriage. It was where Wade's and Mary's granddaughters had been born. They could picture them all now … Allison opening the door and holding out her arms to welcome them and Gail and Sarah, all smiles, running out to meet them, their long, dark hair flying free in the breeze. "Nana Mary, Grampa Wade!" They could see their big smiles, hear the giggles, and almost feel their arms circling Mary's waist and then reaching out to hug Wade. It caught Mary totally off guard. "I see what you mean, Son," she said to Jess.

The moment passed and they went into the house, which seemed so open and cheerful. The slight scent of cinnamon was still there. Once they were unpacked and settled in their bedroom, Mary asked if they should telephone Sylvia and Bill.

"Yes, I promised we would call as soon as we you had made yourselves at home here," Jess said. They dialed the number and made plans to get together the next day. Mary asked Jess to show them some of his sketches. Soon, they were all trying to politely "swallow" yawns, which made them laugh and decide it was time to get some sleep.

When Jess woke the next morning, the clock beside the bed read 6:00a.m. He showered and dressed, picked up the Washington Post from the front steps and went out on the patio with a cup of coffee to read and to watch the sun rise.

His parents joined him about 8:00 and after a leisurely breakfast, they made the beautiful drive from Montclair to Manassas. The mountains and forests delighted Mary and Wade, who were used to the flat topography of southwestern Florida. The thirty-minute drive seemed very short.

Bill and Sylvia welcomed them warmly; Bill invited Wade to go to the garage workshop with him to look at some of the new models and plans he had of the planes that would be doing the work of detecting and predicting the weather. Mary and Sylvia were already involved in a conversation on the topic of homeowner associations, which they had been discussing by mail for the past couple months.

Jess spent some time answering some urgent business emails on his computer and then joined Wade and Bill in Bill's study.

The rest of the visit with his parents flew by, with different activities every day. They spent part of each day with Sylvia and Bill. When Jess had work to do, the four parents would do some sightseeing in the District or in the beautiful Maryland or Virginia countryside. They met each night for dinner and there were always stories to tell of past and present adventures.

The day before Wade and Mary flew back to Florida, Jess drove everyone to see the one remaining empty lot in Montclair that had been part of Bill and Sylvia's wedding gift to Jess and Allison. They got out and walked around beautiful Lake Montclair that bordered the large lot. "This is a lot with one of the best views in the community," Jess told them, and everyone agreed. "It was Allison's and my plan to build a summer home (or permanent home) here for you, Mom and Dad."

Mary burst into tears. Wade put his arm around her to comfort her. Mary looked around the circle of the people she loved most in the world. "Oh, Jess. That will be lovely," she said. "There will come a time when we will want to live much closer to all of you ... our family." Wade agreed. Jess hugged them both and said, "OK, so when you get back to Florida I'll expect to see some ideas soon of what you would like the house to look like. The lot is one of the last ones in here that would accommodate a ranch style, one-story house, just in case that's what you would like. But it doesn't have to be." His mother almost jumped with happiness. "That's exactly what I've always dreamed of. A house all on one floor with a water view!!"

They all chatted happily about the prospect of being neighbors as they parted for the evening. Jess knew he would have them as neighbors as soon as he could get a house built for them. He was thrilled at the prospect.

PART II

SID

Chapter Eleven
Sid's Parents

Una and David Harkness 1942-1954

Una had been the only child of parents who died in an automobile accident when Una was 17 and a freshman at Cornell. She was able to care for herself, and with the funds that had been provided for her education, she continued her studies through to the doctoral level and earned a fellowship to continue studying and working in the chemistry department at Cornell.

Her mother and father had believed that a child's intellect must be developed without interference from such distractions as dolls and toys. They had not wasted any time on affection, either. They had provided her with language tutors and music theory teachers from the age of three. Books had been her entertainment. She could read in English and in French by age 4. She enjoyed art history books the most at that age, but was not given canvas or paints or a sketchpad. Her intellect was what was being developed. Her childhood was devoted to reading about, rather than experiencing, life. Her focus as a teenager was on choosing an appropriate university for furthering her studies.

David's parents had divorced soon after he was born. His father had taken an ambassadorship somewhere in Europe. His mother had left David in the care of an elderly maiden aunt and had gone her separate way. Aunt Josephine thus became the surrogate parent of David. She had inherited a sizeable amount of money from her parents, and she had saved most of it. She was a tall, large-boned woman with a pleasant face, graying hair, and a genuine smile. She had loved a man who went off to war and never returned. She kept a faded, tear-stained photograph of him in her King James Bible in the 1st Chapter of the Book of Ruth.

His Aunt Josephine had hired a nanny to see to David's needs as an infant. The same woman continued to care for him thereafter. Her name was Doris, and she was a kind person who came from a desperately impoverished family. Doris was grateful to be living in a household where she had access to her own tiny but comfortable bedroom, two uniforms, regular meals, and a monthly allowance of $5.00 in cash. She liked the regularity of her daily routine of bathing, dressing, and feeding the baby, taking him out for a walk, and seeing that he was safe and quiet throughout the days and nights. She would dress him in one of his little rompers and take him downstairs to visit his Aunt Josephine every day after his nap. David was a bright, outgoing child, and was an interesting diversion to his aunt and her friends. She was usually just finishing a bridge game or a meeting with her garden club or literature club. The ladies would chatter away to David and want to hold him on their laps. So he was acknowledged and made to feel appreciated.

At about age 3, Aunt Josephine hired a tutor named Miss Sherman to live in the servants' wing with them and to begin David's formal education. This gave Doris an hour of free time every morning while David was in the school room. She would do the laundry as usual and then several times a week would be sent out to walk to the library with a list of books for the librarian. She carried a cloth sack full of any books to be returned and exchanged for the new list. The library was a beautiful old building with a stone front and white columns. It made Doris feel like a student when she entered the building and walked past the shelves filled with so many, many books on her way to the main desk. She would hand the librarian the sack and the list. The librarian would send a young assistant out to scurry around the stacks and gather together the newly requested list. Then the librarian, Miss White, would smile and hand the sack back to Doris, and she would be on her way.

After David's lesson and before lunch, Doris would take him for a walk in the park. There they would see mothers and other children. David could speak very clearly and distinctly, but he was a bit shy. He didn't join in the games that the others played, running and chasing a ball, or playing hide-and-seek. He smiled at the others, but he stayed close to Doris and talked to her. Walking home, he liked to pass the ice cream store which advertised homemade ice cream and had a colorful picture in the window drawn by a local artist of two little bears eating ice cream cones at a picnic in the country. David was a contented and happy child who had never experienced a picnic.

When David was about five, Miss Sherman began to take him to the library to pick out and carry home his own (guided) choice of books. He devoured books on all subjects. At the age of 10 he announced his goal of reading every book in the library. That was when Aunt Josephine hired an instructor named Mr. Barnes from the university to come to their house twice a week to introduce additional subjects such as advanced math and science to her nephew. David was ecstatic. He loved the logic of science and the analysis of various scientific methods. Within two years he was walking up the hills to the campus for his lessons and was using the labs with some skill. He was still quiet and shy, but he was intent on advancing in the areas of science and mathematics. His first love was physics, and he pursued it with a vengeance. His aunt decided to have him attend a private high school, hoping that would encourage him to make some social connections. David was most comfortable in the company of his professors and academic instructors and never really adapted to interacting with his own age group in social situations. He excelled in his high school studies, and was accepted for early admission at all of the Ivy League universities. In his four years at Cornell, he took an accelerated course and finished the requirement for the bachelor's and master's degrees. He then was given a fellowship and went on to acquire a PhD while teaching at his alma mater. The Physics Department was intent on adding him to their faculty. He accepted with pleasure, and began a satisfying career in the field of study that he loved.

David and Una met by chance at a faculty tea which was one of the few events at which attendance by the science faculty was required. Each of them was standing uncomfortably, sipping soda water, amid the crowd of faculty and graduate students who had gathered for cocktails in the lounge prior to the formal dinner. The press of people approaching the bar jostled Una's arm and pushed her into David. He expertly recovered his balance, looked over at her shyly, and smiled. "Oh, pardon me, I'm so sorry," she said. "It's OK. We're in an unruly mob," he smiled again in reassurance.

He glanced over and saw some chairs along the wall. "Shall we take cover over there?" he asked, pointing to the chairs. They sat and watched the crowd pressing in, obtaining drinks, and surging back. "I'm not good at things like parties," Una confessed. "Nor am I," David answered. "I never know what to say or do. So I just freeze in place." He was thinking how unusual this interaction with Una was. He seldom spoke to anyone except for the necessary limited conversation with his students. And here he was sitting and chatting with a young scientist who was a female!

What was the attraction between these two brilliant scientists? They seemed an unlikely pair. Both were unremarkable in appearance and in mannerisms. Yet, as time went on, they were somehow drawn to each other. Una was slender and stood very straight to show off her five-feet-five inches in height to advantage. She spoke little, being more comfortable with reading to herself than with speaking aloud. She appeared to be rather drab and unimaginative. Actually, she was brilliant intellectually, eager to please, but had not had any training in developing social skills. She knew her subject matter, but really had no sparkle in her personality. She repressed every impulse to reach out to others.

David was a short, bookish young man with wire-rimmed glasses containing strong lenses that magnified his soft brown eyes. His black hair was combed straight back to cover an area that was balding ever so slightly. One thing that David thoroughly enjoyed was working in the lab at the university. He was a man of few words and also preferred reading to speaking. He provided his students with reading assignments and written handouts daily, and he did very little lecturing. He was quite shy.

The two exchanged names and departments and ended up spending the evening together, almost entirely in a companionable silence. They enjoyed it so much that they made a date to meet for lunch on campus mid-week.

Lunch on Wednesdays became a regular event after that. Their routine was to take turns bringing a book to the cafeteria. The person bringing the book would have prepared a summary of some key point and the arguments supporting that point. If Una brought the book and the summary, then David would read it to himself and study it as they ate. After lunch, they would go to one of the lounges where he would write a reply and his own conclusions. Una would read this and write a reply in return. They spoke little, but they were totally absorbed in each other's brilliant analyses of scientific principles. They had much in common. Like David, Una had completed her PhD studies in record time and was part of the science faculty in the Chemistry Department.

They expanded their social interaction to include attendance at the Sunday afternoon classical string-quartet musical events on campus. They would also meet during the week in the library and read independently, but sitting near each other. David would walk Una back to her faculty apartment after these meetings. Conversation was minimal. Their being together became a comfortable habit.

The subject of marriage came up after they had been following this routine for a little over two years. David proposed that they marry, and Una accepted. Their plan was that they would be contributing to the necessary conservation of resources on the planet if they shared quarters and that they would be contributing to the prosperity of the country if they purchased a modest, efficiently engineered house. They agreed that they felt affection for each other in a fraternal sense and that they could sincerely commit themselves to a shared lifestyle of living in harmony together. They further agreed that they would continue their careers to advance scientific discovery. For this reason, they would not produce children to add to the burden of the growing strain on planetary resources, and they would care for each other compassionately and faithfully. They sealed the bargain with a smile and a handshake.

They pooled their financial resources to buy a desirable lot that would be a wise investment. They contracted for a modest home to be built with a bedroom for each of them and one for the child they planned to adopt. When the house was completed, the marriage ceremony was performed by a Justice of the Peace who provided the required witness. David regretted that his Aunt Josephine could not be with them at the wedding, but she had entered a whole new exciting phase of her life. After his graduation, Aunt Josephine had sold her house, given David a gift of cash to put aside for his retirement, and had gone off to travel the world and enjoy herself. She was, at last, a free spirit, having adventures in every corner of the world. She and David would always have a reserved affection for each other, but oh how different they were in every other way! David was so grateful for the education and care he had been given by his aunt. He was also grateful that she had let him respond to the world in his own quiet way.

Chapter Twelve
Sid's Arrival, 1954

Sid's arrival was considered a miracle by his adoptive parents. They had saved a considerable sum of money by careful budgeting during their eight years of marriage, and they desperately wanted to be responsible parents and to provide a service to the community by adopting a child who had been unwanted by birth parents. Both Una and David passionately believed that overpopulation was a major problem in the 20th century. They had decided in a brief, but intense discussion before marriage that they would not reproduce and add to this burden. They had studied child-rearing extensively, and they had placed their names on a local list of adults desiring to adopt. They worked and saved for those eight years and adopted a newborn little boy in 1954.

The brown-eyed infant with a light dusting of dark hair who was placed in Una's arms was exactly what they had anticipated. Here was a miniature human whom they could form into a well-educated, contributing member of society. They entered into raising the boy methodically, with great determination. They were armed with every possible textbook and scientific study that was available to intellectually advanced persons. They were purposeful and methodical in their approach to his nurturing and care. Una had initially taken a year off from her position at Cornell so that she could give little Sidney Armstrong Harkness her full attention.

His food was weighed and measured and his formula was carefully controlled as to content. He was fed according to a rigid schedule. Every four hours around the clock. Una relied heavily on the Department of Nutrition for advice in this regard. Sid was pre-enrolled at the Cornell Experimental Nursery School as an infant to assure his admission at age 3. Every aspect of their lives was now regulated and adjusted with Sid in mind. Una meticulously kept charts and graphs documenting every detail of their experiment in child rearing.

Una and David, possessors of two lonely souls starving for sustenance, had reached out to each other in the only way they knew how. They had connected through their brilliant minds. They had a unique form of marriage. Now they had a child to raise! Would their intellectual development and connection be enough to sustain them and Sid? They had no expanded frame of reference within which to evaluate or even consider this question.

Sid's first six months were unremarkable. His parents noticed that he did not smile, but they accepted that because they themselves were not effusive people. He did not cry much, either. They attributed this to the fact that they had organized his schedule so well that he experienced no trauma or discord. He lived a perfectly regulated life. They would have liked to have him make eye contact with them, but Sid kept to himself and spent most of his time looking silently in the direction of his feet. He learned to sit by himself at 6 months, but the smiling, cooing, and babbling that were on the checklist in "My Baby's First Seven Years," were not on his list of goals achieved.

They began to be concerned when, at seven months as he started to pull himself to a standing position, he would furiously bang his head against the bars of his crib. When he was lifted gently from the crib, he would wiggle furiously to be released from his mother's arms. If Una set him on a blanket on the floor, he would sit silently for hours. She reluctantly tried an experiment in which she would sit beside him on the blanket, but allow Sid free rein to do as he wished. It was only when she reached out tentatively to stroke his soft hair or to touch his smooth cheek that he would react. He would shudder and recoil from her touch. She would abruptly and guiltily withdraw her hand and either sit in silence or stand and go elsewhere in the room. He made no sound, but his expression changed to one which she could only describe as loathing. At age 13 months, he began walking rather aimlessly around the living room. He began to display a facial expression that was a sort of disdainful, inward grin, more like a sneer. It was not directed at any one person or object. Sid lived inside a world of his own creation, it appeared. He was compliant, but self-absorbed in eating, sleeping, and toilet training. He was nonresponsive to overtures of attention and interaction. Una and David had no outside activities. They lived apart from campus social life and kept to themselves. They had no models of child rearing, and they relied solely on referencing scholarly studies and books for guidance.

Una and David discussed Sid's withdrawal and related behaviors and tried to come up with sensible solutions. David thought the boy might be a scholar who would suddenly burst into the production of whole sentences at a young age.

Una was concerned. None of this was occurring, and with each passing day she became more convinced that it would not.

Una doubted that Sid would be ready for the rigorous intellectual training that she and David had received as children. She hoped that they would not be forced into any social situations where this might be revealed to others.

The desire to cuddle her child in her arms and to sing to him, read to him, and exchange smiles with him never arose, as she had no idea of that side of parenting.

Una and David started taking little Sid for longer walks in his stroller, around the neighborhood and to the parks. By the time he was two, they would let him out of the stroller to play on the grass or in the sandbox. Sid remained uninterested in his surroundings with one exception. He was fascinated by living things such as worms and caterpillars and lizards. He would smile his sneering grin and deftly dismember the helpless little creatures. Una and David were appalled. They called the pediatrician to ask what to do. He suggested that they read stories about small animals to Sid to give him an appreciation for them. He also asked if Sid had any stuffed animals to play with, to which he could develop loving attachments. A live pet would be out of the question until the child displayed less savage tendencies toward animals.

Sid seemed to like the inanimate stuffed toys better than he did living beings. He was given a little elephant, a bear, a pig, and a duck as well as a toy dog and a cat. The elephant was his favorite. He carried it around by its tail wherever he went and liked to throw it at the other animals. His sneer was soon accompanied by a sort of laugh that did not sound at all cheerful. He also started to speak. His words came out somewhat explosively as commands: "Water!" "Eat!" "Out!" David and Una gently encouraged him to continue to speak by cheerfully obeying each of these commands.

When Sid was three years of age, Una decided to take him for a visit to the campus nursery school. She and David explained to Sid where they were going in detail. They drove past the building on campus that contained the school, and they walked there on a Sunday, exploring the grounds, pushing Sid in his stroller. They showed Sid the playground in the back. He showed no interest in it. "Eat!" he demanded. They went home to have Sunday dinner.

Una walked to the building housing the nursery school, pushing Sid in the stroller on the appointed day and were met at the door of her office by the director, Mrs. Louise Hollister, a petite woman who exuded an air of both competence and compassion. She greeted Una warmly, referring to her by her professional title as "Dr. Harkness." She squatted down to Sid's level, extended her hand and said, "Good Morning, Sidney." Sid turned away with a glowering look. As soon as Una lifted him out of the stroller, he sat down on the floor outside the office. When Una reached over gently to help him up, he recoiled and did what he had never done before, he screamed shrilly and eerily and would not stop. That was when the dam of resistance and fear and denial inside of Una broke with such force that it almost knocked her off her feet. She burst into tears and wrenching sobs. Her beautiful, kind face collapsed in confusion and grief.

Mrs. Hollister firmly lifted the screaming child and carried him into the office. Setting him down on the carpet, she closed the door and invited Una to sit in a comfortable chair next to the one she pulled over. "Let's let him express his feelings," Mrs. Hollister advised. Una felt a mixture of guilt, embarrassment, and concern, but she accepted the advice. They ignored the child for the moment as the mother's tears flowed and Una poured out the heartbreaking story of her brief journey through motherhood.

Tissues were brought to their side of the desk. Mrs. Hollister took both of Una's hands in hers, gently raised Una's chin, and looked into her tear filled eyes. "That's not the way it's supposed to be, but it is the way it sometimes happens," she told Una. "The vital truth to remember – always, no matter what happens – is that you have done nothing wrong and everything right!"

Una nodded, and her sobs began to lessen. "He is our son. We have tried so hard to do everything right. How can we do better? We want so much to be good parents!"

"I don't think there is an easy answer to that question. I can suggest a first step, but I have no solutions."

"Oh, Mrs. Hollister, please tell me how to get started!"

"Please call me Louise."

"Thank you … and… call me Una."

"Una, there is a study … well there are always a number of studies going on here in child development. There is one now for which I believe Sid would be eligible, from what you have told me. You and your husband would have to apply. Sid would be tested." Seeing the anxious look on Una's face, she quickly added, "No, don't worry, it is not an achievement test. It is a test of where he is emotionally and psychologically. The children who are accepted for the study will be eligible for various treatment modalities that will be offered to parents at the conclusion of the test."

Throughout this exchange between the two women, Sid continued the blood curdling screams. It was as if he had found a new voice with which to express his opinion of the world and those with whom he associated. They were not screams of physical pain. It was as if they rose from the depths of his soul, and he was crying out in frustration at some form of imprisonment.

"Before you leave here today, I want you to meet two people, Una." Louise Hollister stepped into the next room for a moment and spoke with her secretary. When she returned, she offered Una a glass of water. Una was so moved by the fact that Louise not only accepted her and her wild son just as they were, but that she seemed to have some answers to the dilemma that had plagued them for the past three years.

Within a few minutes, there was a knock on the door, and a young woman was welcomed into, Former friends and colleagues seemed to light up, the room. She was of medium height and wore a lab coat and carried a clipboard containing a pad of paper. She had short-cropped black hair, brown eyes, and a wide smile. "Good morning, Peggy," Louise said. "Dr. Harkness, this is Peggy Abbot, who is a doctoral candidate and the leading research associate on the project I was describing to you. I hope you will exchange telephone numbers so that an appointment can be arranged to have Sidney interviewed and tested for the project. I think it would be best for you to arrange to meet both parents together, Peggy. Both are Dr. Harkness – Una and David."

Peggy Abbot extended her hand and made a note of the names and phone numbers. Una found herself smiling unexpectedly in response to the warmth and hospitality radiating from the younger woman. They set a time to meet her at her lab the next day. Una would confirm with David and then telephone Peggy or her lab assistant.

Una felt better already in spite of the almost supernatural wailing just across the room. Peggy said goodbye to Una and to Louise and called out loudly to be heard over the crying, "Goodbye, Sidney!" Sid suddenly stopped mid-scream and was silent.

The next knock at the door was from a woman who Una judged was close to her own age. Again, the warm greeting by Louise Hollister and the introduction. "Dr. Harkness, I would like you to meet Dr. Karen Wilson."

Una took Karen Wilson's hand and was, as if by a magnetic force drawing her in, attracted to Karen's wide, friendly smile and sparkling blue eyes. The woman's hair was arranged in a long braid that extended halfway down her back. She was slender and built like an accomplished athlete. Una usually felt awkward being introduced to a new person, but she liked Karen immediately and, remarkably, felt totally at ease.

"My field is biology, and my husband, Paul, is in the Engineering School," Karen volunteered.

"My husband, David, is in the Physics Department and I'm in Chemistry, well that is, I was before I became a mother," Una replied suddenly looking down at her shoes.

"I'm not working either," Karen said. "We have a child who requires a lot of extra attention, so teaching is out of the question, maybe for a long time."

Una's defenses had sprung into action again, but, hearing this, she relaxed a little. "I'm finding that I don't have the flexibility that I did before Sid came into our lives," she volunteered, looking up at Karen again, almost apologetically.

Louise intervened, "I brought you two together, Una and Karen, because I think you can both use some moral support in your struggle." Una blushed and looked down, but did not try to stop the conversation. "I hope you two will become acquainted," Louise continued. "A friend is essential on anyone's journey through life. A friend is essential in the situation that you are facing and must continue in. I would be so pleased if you would both consider this opportunity and exchange telephone numbers and maybe plan to meet for some conversation in the near future."

The two women looked at each other, and Una took out a paper and pencil. Karen did the same. They exchanged information. Una described where their house was located, and Karen's eyes opened even wider as she said, "I live on the corner of Triphammer and Upland Road."

"But that's just a block and a half from our house!" Una gasped with delight. "Talk about things that are meant to be!"

Louise smiled slightly and made no comment. Had she known this when she arranged the meeting?

Chapter Thirteen
Metamorphosis

The study began with Sid and ten others as subjects. Una and David were so relieved to be working with a team of concerned experts in the field of child development. Their lives were completely changed. Any problems or anxieties they were feeling about their son could be noted, charted by them, and kept for the future discussion phase of the study. The data gathering was moving along rapidly. Every Wednesday Una would walk to the campus with Sid and wait while he was observed in a room with three other children his age. She and the other parents were able to see what was happening through a one-way window that looked like a mirror to the children on the other side. There were two graduate-student faculty members, Peggy and a young man named Nelson, who would make detailed observational records of the movements and vocalizations of each child. These were later coded and the results analyzed.

Una could see clearly that Sid was not at all interested in the other children. Nor was he reaching for the colorful, appealing toys. There were shelves within reach of all the children that contained trucks, boats, blocks, dolls, stuffed animals, and children's books. Sid sat on the floor and stared at his feet. The other children did not approach him. They interacted with the toys. After two weeks of observation at this level, Peggy and Nelson took turns approaching the children and attempting to play with the toys in both a parallel-play situation and then an interactive session. As Peggy sat down very close to Sid with some large building blocks, he looked at her with a startled glance and then began to scream. He screamed so loudly that his face turned red and his body shook. He literally howled in rage and began to beat his fists in the air. Peggy spoke to him softly, but he did not waver in his protest. She then shouted at him with a smile on her face: "Sidney, please stop!" He abruptly stopped, and looked at her in amazement. She made notes as did Nelson. Then she approached Sid again with a toy truck and said loudly, "Sid, here is a toy for you!" Sid reached out his hands and took it and held it close to his body. When the hour was up, they had to let him take the truck home with him as he would not let go of it and held it in an iron grip.

Before they left the campus, they were taken to one of the labs where an audiologist told Una that they would like to attempt to test Sid's hearing. She agreed, signed the permission form, and the examiner performed some preliminary tests by speaking to Sid from beside, behind, and in front of him. He spoke very clearly in a voice that Una found to be way too loud. He then told Sid in the same high volume voice that they were going to play a game. As he spoke, he handed the child a ball. To Una's amazement, Sid grabbed for it with the ferocity of a wild animal being offered a piece of meat. He held it close to his body next to the truck. The examiner then approached Sid on the right, speaking softly. He asked gently if Sid would like to throw the ball. Sid immediately began to scream and went rigid, though he still clutched the truck and the ball.

"I think we have discovered part of the problem," the examiner said, returning to his desk chair. Your son has a loss of hearing in both ears and a vision problem in his right eye. He cannot hear words that are spoken softly. He is frightened when someone he doesn't recognize approaches his right side because he can neither hear them nor see them clearly, but he senses their presence and is startled and frightened. This is especially true when he is in unfamiliar surroundings and cannot recognize any landmarks. He is familiar with the rooms in your house, and is used to the vague images that he perceives there, but he is disoriented and visibly upset by other locations.

We will have to do some tests of both vision and hearing. Since he obviously can't read letters or speak about symbols to us, we will have to do the best we can to give him improved eyesight and hearing. We'll have the ophthalmologist take a look. I don't want to upset the boy by moving him to yet another room, so I'll see if Dr. Benson can come to us. He dialed a number and soon a young doctor joined them. He sat on the floor in front of Sid and looked into his eyes. "There's a cataract in the right eye," he said. "It's distorting his vision, and that's why his eye looks so cloudy."

Una asked that they telephone David. He walked over from his office and joined them. The diagnosis was explained by the two doctors and David asked for their recommendations. Dr. Benson spoke first and described a new procedure that had first been done in 1949 in England by a young ophthalmologist named Harold Ridley. It involved the insertion into the eye following removal of the cataract of what was called an intraocular lens. The procedure was now, in the late 1950s, being successfully implemented at the Wills Eye Clinic in Philadelphia, PA. Dr. Benson thought there would be interest at that clinic in looking into Sid's case. If it could be accepted as a case study, upon the recommendation of the Cornell team, the cost would be minimal and the result would be the best possible.

Further inquiry and exploration of all aspects of the surgery and its outcomes followed over the next few weeks. Finally, in August of 1959 when Sid was almost 4 years old, the preparations had been made and Una and Sid travelled to Philadelphia with a nurse who had been selected by Dr.

Benson. The surgery was televised for education purposes and recorded. This was a new idea, also originally conceived by Harold Ridley, MD, whose brilliant pioneering work had been done in England at the world renowned Moorfields Eye Hospital and at St. Thomas Hospital in London.

The operation proceeded without incident. Since being fitted with two hearing aids, Sid already seemed like a different child. He loved the hearing aids and called them "ears." The first thing he did upon opening his eyes after a night's sleep or a nap was to ask for his "Ears!" He had begun to speak almost immediately upon receiving them, and now had a vocabulary of about 200 words. He spoke in complete sentences and added new words to his vocabulary at a rapid pace. Una and David hoped that with the correction of his vision he would be able to enter the nursery school and would learn to enjoy being with other children.

The day of the removal of the cataract and the implanting of the intraocular transplant, Una and the nurse took turns sitting with Sid and making sure that he did not pull at the bandage covering his eye. Sid was sedated, and he was remarkably docile and cooperative. They remained at the hospital until the doctor was ready to remove the bandage. David had finished the summer term and joined them as soon as he could. Sid was happy to see his father and immediately asked, "Daddy, read a story?" David was moved almost to tears every time he heard his son address him in a loving way after all the years of silence and withdrawal. He was delighted to read stories anytime.

Sid talked to the nurses, and they all loved the brave little dark-haired angelic boy. They found excuses to stop by the room to see him and to bring him little treats such as paper and crayons and a coloring book. The day the bandage was removed, Sid reacted with fear at first. The bright clear light was disorienting to him. He was used to distorted shadows. Now his eyes had to adjust to working together and no longer needed to try to accomplish the impossible task of focusing when one was malfunctioning and confusing the other.

Sid ran up and down the corridor of the hospital and did not bump into anything. His fear of walking, running, and of having distorted images of people approach him was gone. He was free to be a little boy and to enjoy life fully for the first time.

Una sobbed with joy as she observed him. Her heart sang as Sid ran into his father's arms and gave him a bear hug. This was the little boy they had wanted for so long. Una believed, at last, that prayers are heard and answered.

Back in Ithaca, Sid was accepted by Louise Hollister as a student in the nursery-school class. He started in September, and he made a good adjustment to being with other children. Sid still did not interact with the children, but he tolerated them and had no objection to sitting quietly in the classroom or on the playground and amusing himself with a book, a puzzle, or, if outdoors, with a plant or an insect. While Sid was in school each day, Una would finish her housework and then walk down the hill to visit Karen Wilson. Karen and her husband Paul were not as fortunate as she and David.

Their four-year old son, Robbie, had been born with spina bifida and would always be confined to a wheelchair. He was a small boy with a pale face, brown eyes, and black wavy hair. His dark, friendly eyes looked out from under thick lashes. He had an other-worldly look, and was a brilliant, avid reader. His slight frame was frail, and his facial features had a pinched appearance, but his spirit was a thing of beauty. He was so considerate of his parents and of any guests. He tired easily, but never complained.

Regular school attendance would not be possible for him, but he loved to learn and his parents took his education very seriously. They already had a tutor for him who came three times a week for an hour at a time to teach reading and piano. Those were the subjects that Karen and her husband chose as the most interesting to Robbie. He was an excellent pianist and could play any piece perfectly once he had heard it performed. His current wheelchair had been designed, with the help of his father, so that the seat could be raised and lowered into several comfortable positions. When he was seated in it, and the control lever was engaged, Robbie could easily reach the piano keyboard. The family had a combination console radio/record player so that Robbie could enjoy hearing classical music as well as popular tunes. Robbie reminded Una of a miniature grown up.

Robbie was delightful, and Karen and her husband loved him beyond measure.

Una and Karen would sit and talk and be entertained at intervals by Robbie. Sometimes, in good weather, Karen would wheel Robbie in his little wheelchair and walk with Una to the campus to pick up Sid from nursery school. They both remembered the days when Una would have to transport Sid in his stroller because he was so afraid of walking and could not tell them why. The transformation of Sid had been truly miraculous, and Karen was glad for her friend. Una was very shy and had never had a close friend like Karen. She reveled in this discovery and found that it gave her a whole new perspective on life. They each had both a vegetable and a flower garden, they loved scientific study and reading, they exchanged recipes, and they enjoyed the rhythm of and maintaining a home and raising their children.

When Robbie was born, Karen had made the decision to make his life as wonderful as was possible. She gladly gave up her teaching career, her service within various worthwhile causes, and found herself isolated from friends who continued on the path she once had traveled. Former friends and colleagues seemed to "erase" her from their busy calendars.

She had been so lonely, and the friendship she now shared with Una meant the world to her. Sid didn't actually play with Robbie or interact with him, but he would sit in one of the child-sized chairs at the little table that had belonged to Karen when she was a child and work on jigsaw puzzles or look at picture books. Sid spoke only when necessary. He smiled in a detached way at adults, especially when he wanted something that only they could provide. Una and David overlooked his sometimes-disconcerting ways. They were just glad that their son could appear in public without misbehaving and that he could communicate through speech and could achieve at the same level academically as his peers.

Chapter Fourteen
Sid Learns to Control His World

Although Sid's life clearly had improved, his attitude about other people had not. In fact, Sid found others to be annoying." He thought of most of them as substandard or defective in some way. His experiments in dismembering insects and small animals had shown him that he had a power over living things that set him apart from other human beings. He attributed much of his skill to the special powers of his enhanced eye.

His mother was especially annoying, with her sweet, gentle voice and her unconditional acceptance of his every word and action. His father was somewhat better. But he, too, was not really a challenge. As for Robbie, Sid found himself strongly attracted to the child, yet he was frightened by him.

He felt drawn to Robbie in a way that seemingly thrilled him, but that seemed to deplete Sid's sense of power over others. He saw this as the expression of a weakness in himself that excited and dismayed him at the same time. He wanted, in some strange way, to become one with Robbie so that he could possess Robbie's natural gifts for music, and art, and literature. He wanted this with a vengeance. He obsessed on how he could achieve it, what plan of action would be necessary, and what the consequences would be. Finally, he had a plan. Robbie would not merge with him willingly, so there would have to be an intermediate step.

Robbie's fifth birthday was approaching. He had recovered sufficiently from an open wound near the base of his sensitive spine that had become infected, to make possible the planning of a birthday celebration. Sid and all of the 10 children in his class were invited to Robbie's house for the party on a sunny Saturday afternoon in April.

The party was held on the patio, but the little guests were invited onto the side lawn for a modified game of croquet in which the wooden balls were rolled by hand in the direction of each wicket instead of using mallets. This gave Robbie an equal chance with the other guests. The lawn was bordered by a sidewalk that led to the mailbox and eventually to the street in front of the house. Karen and Una were both present helping the children play the game and chasing after any runaway balls.

Sid's opportunity came when Una had to go into the house to take one of the children to the bathroom. Karen was distracted in helping a couple children with the game, when Sid, who had been carefully watching Robbie from the sidelines, focusing on him with his special eye that he believed gave him magical powers, quietly stepped up behind Robbie's wheelchair. Sid quickly unlocked the wheels and swiveled it so that it was heading down the sidewalk in the direction of the street.

No one was watching as the game was at a crucial point when the winners would be decided and prizes awarded. He gave it a mighty push and then sat on the grass near Karen and watched the game with great attention. Suddenly, there was a crash and a scream. They all looked at once and saw with horror that the wheelchair had slammed hard into the mailbox at the end of the sidewalk and was being catapulted to a great height and hurled into the street. Una ran out of the house just at that moment and joined the scream of the others and the pounding feet that rushed to rescue Robbie.

Robbie was lying motionless in a tangle of crushed metal. His neck was at an odd angle as if it had been twisted around. His mother ran and tried to extricate the lifeless body of her beloved child from the wreckage. Una gathered the children together, took them inside the house, and called the emergency number on the telephone. Then she called each of the children's parents to report that there had been a terrible accident, that none of their children had been involved, but that the parents should come as quickly as possible.

Sid stood placidly at the front window, his heart beating rapidly, watching every move that took place outside. He felt an exhilaration beyond anything he had ever experienced. He understood that outwardly he looked the same. No one but he would know the secret that he had just added a new and valuable part to himself. He had taken the life from Robbie out of the broken, useless body and added the best of Robbie to what was inside himself. He wanted to weep with joy at the beauty of it! He would have to be careful not to act too happy. He knew instinctively that no one among his friends, family, or school associates would understand. He would have to listen to them and watch carefully, as he always did, to observe what he was to say and do so that he could keep his secret.

For the next two hours there was complete bedlam. The story had to be told countless times from Karen's point of view. That somehow Robbie's chair had not been locked after his last turn at rolling the croquet ball, that he had somehow started rolling down the sidewalk, and that, of course, he was too frightened to react at first, and helpless to stop the forward momentum. The parents whisked their children away and Karen and Una waited for their husbands to join them. When David and Paul arrived, the story was retold. Sid sat in silence and relived their version with mute satisfaction. He sat at the little table for a while and played with some of Robbie's games and puzzles. He felt satisfied and at peace for the first time in many months. It was as if a fire that raged inside him had been tamed and brought under control.

There were funeral plans to be made. The pastor came as soon as he heard. Neighbors shared the news, and people came to the door with casseroles and cookies. Karen and Paul called their families with the devastating news. David suggested that Una take Sid home for his supper and bath and bed as he was sure that this was overwhelming for the little boy. Sid did not tell them that he did not want to leave. Una promised to spend the next day with Karen. They hugged and David ruffled Sid's hair and asked for a goodnight hug. Sid complied and looked as sad as possible.

Sid had a hard time falling asleep that night, because he was still so energized by the experience. He finally drifted off and strangely in his dream that night Robbie was able to walk. He and Sid met in a meadow and smiled at each other and kissed and hugged and stood together so closely that it was as if they were one person. He smiled with great satisfaction in the dream. They had merged, and he knew he was more powerful because of it!

Chapter Fifteen
Get Out of Jail Free

Sid advanced rapidly in school after that, with excellent grades. Once he believed that he had achieved the merger with Robbie, he considered himself to be a gifted student, and acted accordingly. Science and math were his favorite subjects, but he applied himself equally in all areas. His parents were ecstatic that he was consistently on the honor roll all through elementary, junior high, and high school. They also celebrated the fact that an IQ test showed their son to be in the genius range with an IQ of 160.

Sid kept to himself, studied all the time, and in his junior year in high school was offered early admission at any university. For economic reasons, he chose Cornell. Tuition would be free because of his father's position, and he could live at home. He majored in biology as an undergraduate. He loved the sciences, but biology held a special fascination for him because of the experiments that led to the dissection and study of living organisms. He did projects for extra credit and received high honors. Math was another subject of high interest, though not as challenging as science. He excelled at both.

School was fine, but Sid was restless. He wanted more out of life than a degree and a boring job. He definitely did not want to be a teacher. He asked his university advisor if he knew of any interesting part-time jobs in any field that he might apply for. His advisor said he would keep his eyes open, and about a week later Sid found a job description attached to an exam paper when it was returned to him.

The job description stated that the local county probation office was seeking an academically advanced and socially well-adjusted college student who would work as a volunteer to interview teenaged boys who had been arrested for felony grade crimes but who were in the 15-17-year-old age bracket and could therefore be sentenced to prison terms in medium to maximum security prisons in New York State if they were found to be guilty. Those who were adjudicated "not guilty" would need to be monitored and probably granted probation.

His job would be to take notes and type the background summaries of each of the young men. He went to the courthouse, applied for the job and began work within a week. He had to be screened first with fingerprinting and letters of reference from teachers and persons active in the community. He was considered to be very mature at age 20 and to be a superior student. His references were excellent.

The best part of the job, as far as Sid was concerned, was that he was able to meet the subjects in person and interview them. He had put all of his attention on his studies through high school and college and had no social life. This job opened up a whole new world to him. Meeting with the teenagers who had taken risks and had been caught, brought to the surface feelings that had been lying dormant within him. He found he was physically attracted to several of the clients. This surprised him a bit. He had never been attracted to girls. To him, they were just another form of biological specimen. Some of the young men with their rippling muscles and firm physiques were definitely turning on parts of his neural network that he had not realized could be activated. There were also the quiet, withdrawn, wounded boys who brought forth feelings within him of wanting to dominate them and make them strong.

Could he merge with them in an innovative way by somehow surrounding them with the power of his personality and making them love, even idolize him for his wisdom and courage? He found himself dreaming of some of the young men and longing to merge with them as he had so many years before with Robbie, but in an even more exciting way. Pressure was building within him. It was accelerating to the level of a demand. As graduation from Cornell approached, he applied himself to the task of finding a lucrative vocation and to focusing on the possibilities unleashed by the volunteer work.

The boys were almost all from sad family situations of poverty and neglect. There were often more children in the family than the parents could afford to support. This led to the teenagers roaming in gangs, stealing cigarettes, gum, beer, etc. from gas stations. When they were caught, they had usually sold the stolen goods and had no money to pay for what was missing. They were in dead-end situations. After interviewing about 30-40 of these hapless youths, a plan was formed in Sid's mind, a plan urgently driven by his emotional hunger.

He was not interested in staying in his hometown. He was determined to go elsewhere and craft a life that would suit him. There would be no fellowships or professorships for him. He would follow his heart, now that he could see where it was leading. The young criminals were unwanted by their families for the most part. They were just so much excess baggage to society. They were seldom employable for more than a month or two. They worked to stay out of jail and to accumulate a few dollars they could use to buy a bus ticket to anywhere but where they were. In the new surroundings, they would find a way to take something that they could sell to buy food for a week or two and would then be back in the "criminal justice system." Their crimes would gradually accelerate and would lead them to prison terms and a dead-end in life. What if these young men could be employed in a profession that provided them with food, clothing, shelter, economic security as well as a substantial guaranteed income for Sid?

He began to carefully and methodically work out the details in his mind. He must be patient and wait for the perfect opportunity. Meanwhile, he would focus on accumulating as much money as possible. He read with interest the reports of newly emerging cities along the east coast. One that particularly caught his attention was the Washington D.C. corridor to the north and south of the District. Affluent settlements were springing up in these areas with the promise of the installation of the Metro transportation network. Fairfax County in Virginia was in a real-estate boom, as was Montgomery County in Maryland. The Metro red line was to be extended to Shady Grove.

Chapter Sixteen
The Thrill of the Hunt

The one thing Sid had the most trouble ignoring, and pretending to accept, was his relationship with Una and David. To him, they were the most boring people in the world. They lived an unimaginative, rigorously scheduled and regulated life. They were vigilant as to how they spent every cent. They never went on vacation or went to a movie. They went to the free concerts on campus on Sunday afternoon. He didn't mind sitting and listening to endless string quartets and wind ensembles, as it gave him an accompaniment to his thoughts of how to escape. But he wanted more, much more, than this stultifying, humdrum life. He wanted to activate the power that was rising inside him and was just waiting for a catalyst to ignite it to its full capacity.

As he sat and listened to the classics, he let his thoughts accelerate with the intensity of the music. He pictured the crackling of a fire in the staccato notes. Moving on, he saw smoke rising and filling a room, removing all of the oxygen. As the music rose in a crescendo, he saw the house engulfed in flames, preventing entry by the firefighters. Then there was the final adagio, in which everything proceeded in a slow, graceful, peaceful manner that was musically sweet and sensual. He pictured the charred empty space where the house and his parents had been. He could see it all so clearly! This, he decided, was because of the power of his special eye. He had the power to see what no one else could! He could see where the music was leading him. It was clearly showing him the way to Paradise on earth.

As the music played, he saw that the whole area he inhabited or ever would inhabit was being transformed through another miraculous merger of life and death. It became a scene not of boredom and a meaningless life, but a rebirth of the land, a rising of new life from beneath the ashes of the old. Yes, this was the gift he would give them. It would be a secret and a total surprise. They deserved to glimpse the wonders of a transformed, merged life. He left the concert smiling his distant smile and felt his own version of happiness as he anticipated the future.

Chapter Seventeen
Dream Scheme, Phase One

Sid's graduation summa cum laude from Cornell was celebrated with an economically priced, but delicious, chicken and biscuit dinner hosted by his parents in the cafeteria at Willard Straight Hall. He was scheduled to be interviewed for a position as assistant director of a prestigious mortgage company in Rockville, Maryland a week later. He also had made connections through his volunteer job with the county to be interviewed for a similar position in Maryland. His parents had given him a leather briefcase as a graduation gift. He had saved every penny of his allowance and any Christmas or birthday monetary gifts from childhood, and he had now purchased a car. It was a 1968 Morris Mini Minor that a Cornell professor had bought in England while on sabbatical. Back in the States, he no longer wanted to own a car, as he lived near campus and preferred walking, as did most of the faculty members. Sid bought the car for $1000, and loved it for its compact look and economy. It was very different from the enormous, finned chariots being promoted by U.S. manufacturers.

As he prepared to leave for his new life away from his parents, Sid took a careful look at the fuse box in the basement. The timing had to be perfect in order for the fire to occur in the night when they were both sound asleep. He would set it up just before he left. He would pretend to leave in the early afternoon. He would say goodbye and then drive to an abandoned barn in a heavily wooded area not far from the house. He would park behind it and wait until dark. Then he would return to the house and overload the circuitry. He had studied this process carefully. He would move silently and not leave a trace. He could enter the house without alerting anyone. He had oiled the hinges on the side door and the cellar door so that they made no sound.

He knew his parents' habits well. They went to bed in their separate bedrooms promptly at 9 p.m. They were sleeping soundly by 10:00 and would each get up briefly around 3:00 a.m. to use the bathroom, and then return to a deep sleep until 7:00 the next morning.

At 11 p.m. he silently entered the house, made the adjustment to the fuse box, plugged in the lamp with the defective cord in the basement near the heating vent and waited for the blaze to start. It came forth on schedule. He was mesmerized by it for a moment, but then quickly unplugged the faulty lamp with asbestos gloves and carried it out of the house with him. He made sure the doors were securely locked, having checked to make sure the windows were locked earlier in the day. He walked through the fields to the barn, retrieved his car, threw the lamp in the back seat, and drove at a steady slow speed past the house. It was already ablaze. He went on by and was well on his way through Pennsylvania toward his destination in Maryland by late morning. He had thrown the lamp in a garbage can at a truck stop near Harrisburg. He was feeling excited and almost giddy at the success of his venture. He wondered if all had gone as planned. He would know soon enough.

Sid did not stop for the night, but drove straight through. He was in a state of wakefulness that would not have allowed sleep. He stopped for a sandwich and a cup of coffee a couple times. When he reached Rockville and his hotel, it was close to noon the next day. He went to a phone booth and dialed his parents' number. The operator gave the message that the phone was out of order. He decided to change and have a meal and then go to his new office at the mortgage company. There was a chance someone would try to reach him there. He knew that his father had the number on file in his office at Cornell. It was also possible that some of the files in the house had survived.

Chapter Eighteen
First Day in the Office 1979

Sid took a minute to size up his new employer, who appeared to be distraught. Al Fisher was slight in build with small dark eyes and a face scarred by acne. He paced around in an agitated way, obviously uncomfortable with the news he was obliged to share. His hair was dark brown and was slicked back with some sort of gel. He was neatly dressed in a conservative, expensive three-piece suit and tie. His shoes were wing-tipped cordovans, meticulously polished so that the supple leather shone. Sid decided not to try to put him at ease but to keep him vulnerable by allowing him to be on edge.

The mortgage broker looked at Sid with alarm and then with great sadness motioned him to a chair. "Sit down, Sid," he said kindly. "I have some very sad news for you."

Sid did not sit down. He literally shouted, "What? What's happened? Tell me!"

The broker spoke softly. "I'm afraid there has been a terrible accident. There was a fire … at your home in New York State…."

"My parents! Are my parents OK!?"

"No, Sid. They were both killed by smoke inhalation. The paramedics said that they died almost instantly and didn't suffer."

Sid sank into the offered chair. His heart was racing. He felt such joy and so much power to have facilitated this! He reached into his mental cache of facial expressions. He attached an appropriate look of shock and dismay to his face, made sure Fisher had seen it, and then buried his face in his hands. He kept repeating, "Oh no! Oh no! Mr. Fisher, what shall I do?"

Fisher, murmuring, "Please call me Al," put a hand on Sid's shaking shoulder. "I have taken the liberty of arranging for one of our company cars and a driver to take you back to Ithaca early tomorrow morning so that you can take care of the necessary arrangements. We'll arrange for you to come back here in a week so that you can start work. If you need longer, that can be arranged."

Sid feigned speechlessness. After a few seconds, he murmured in a barely audible voice, "Thank you so much."

"You're welcome, Sid. I'll show you to your office so that you can use the telephone to make any calls. Just as a suggestion, you may want to call your family lawyer first and let him help you with the logistics of this."

"Thank you, Al," Sid gasped, looking stricken.

Sid was shown into a small tidy office with a gray metal desk on which there was an adding machine, a typewriter, and a telephone. He sat down in the swivel chair and called information for the number of the family lawyer. The call was answered at once and soon he was in the efficient hands of Wendell Mosher, Esq. The lawyer had heard of the tragedy and assured Sid that he would take care of the calls to the fire department and the police department to inquire about the status of the death certificates and the coroner's report. As soon as he had that information, they could call the funeral home and make arrangements. He asked Sid where he was, and Sid explained that he was at his office in Rockville, Maryland but that he had arranged to be transported to Ithaca the following day and would be able to meet with Wendell Mosher on the day after that. Meanwhile, he left his number and waited for the call back.

Al and his secretary brought Sid a cup of coffee and a sandwich. He was ravenous, but he didn't want them to know that, so he nibbled at the sandwich very slowly and drained the cup of coffee. The secretary, Sally, brought in a piece of cake also. "We had a birthday cake for one of the girls today," she said. "You're young enough not to worry about calories. Cake is good medicine!"

Sid liked Sally, and he ate all of the cake. Lee Mosher called back and said that the fire inspector had looked over what was left of the house, which wasn't much, and had determined that the fire was an accident. The insurance company had been contacted and would pay for Sid's lodging and expenses. He was to produce an inventory of what had been in the house as to clothing and furnishings. Sid knew that his father had all of that written out. The lawyer confirmed that he had the document in his office safe, along with the wills of both Una and David. The wills made Sid the executor of their estates and made him their sole heir in the event that they died in a common disaster. He also had an insurance policy, their instructions for a funeral and the deeds to their burial plot at Eastlawn Cemetery.

Sid called the designated funeral home and arranged for the bodies to be transported there as soon as he arrived in Ithaca. He called and made a motel reservation and then spoke with Al for a while about the office and what his duties would be. He made sure to have his voice break from grief several times as he listened. He asked to set up some files that day so that he would be ready to start as soon as he was back. Al was pleased with this new, energetic worker, and together they put things in order, working through the afternoon.

The return to Ithaca was anticlimactic. Sid was anxious to have this business over and done with and to be back in Maryland in his office. He could see that the lawyer was handling everything most efficiently. He submitted his travel and lodging expenses to date and arranged for the funeral to be held at the funeral home two days after he arrived back in town. He contacted the dean of his father's department and the few friends the couple had. The funeral was well attended and he received condolences and hugs and reassuring pats on the back from the attendees. The graveside service was brief and arrangements were made for a single, tastefully designed headstone that would list the names of his parents and the dates they had resided on earth.

The lawyer gave him the good news that he would inherit the proceeds from the fire insurance policy, which fully insured the house and contents, and the proceeds from two life insurance policies that were each in the amount of $500,000. He had the stake he had wanted and needed to start his new life. And he had saved his parents from a life of boredom and from an eventual decline in health that would have sunk them into the decrepitude of old age!

He contacted Al Fisher and let him know that he was ready to return. This time, Fisher arranged for him to fly from Ithaca to Washington National Airport, and the company limo picked him up there. He stayed for a few days at a hotel in Rockville, and then signed a lease at an upscale apartment building not far from the office. He was finally home and in complete charge of his life.

Chapter Nineteen
Dream Scheme, Phase Two 1979-1987

Partnership

After eight very successful years of working together, Al Fisher made Sid Harkness an equal partner in the firm of Community Corners Mortgage. Sid had a way of working with clients that Al envied. Al had always been rather shy. He was very good in the side of the business that required preparation of documents and compilation of statistics. He soon found that Sid seemed to adapt, on sight, to each of the many and varied personalities of the clients. He had a way of almost reading their minds and saying what they most wanted to hear. The closings went smoothly and were tension-free. There may have been last-minute glitches, but Sid was able to resolve any problems quickly and with positive results.

Al began to rely more and more on Sid to be at every closing. Al was a man of high ethics and great fairness. He saw that he was asking Sid to bear the burden of keeping the company running flawlessly.

Al made a proposal to Sid that they become partners in the business. Sid paused for a very long minute, pretending to think this over. Al became anxious as the pause extended to three minutes, and Sid appeared to be deep in thought. Al broke the silence (just as Sid had hoped). "How does it sound, Sid? Is there anything else I can do to make the offer more attractive?"

Sid looked thoughtful for just a moment more before answering. He stood up and paced around the room. Stopping across from Al, he pulled a chair over so that they were close together. "The offer is attractive, Al, but I have one concern."

Al immediately answered, "What is it? We can work it out. Just tell me, please!" Sid gloated within. He had Al Fisher just where he wanted him. It was almost too easy. Sid applied an earnest, concerned expression to his face, made the effort to look at Al and plunged in.

"Al, you and I aren't just business associates. We have become friends. I am so grateful for the training and encouragement you've given me. I will be honored to be your partner, but I have one additional request."

Relieved, Al jumped in. "Just name it, Sid."

Sid smiled his odd sideways smile that looked so much like a sneer. "I think if we're going to be partners, we should trust each other enough to assure the company's future by setting up an irrevocable trust, in which each of us names the other as beneficiary, in case one of us dies before the other."

Al laughed aloud in relief. "Of course we should do that, Sid! We don't have wives or children. We'll have the lawyer prepare all the papers and cover the bases in one shot!"

They both stood, shook hands vigorously, and the deal was made.

The papers were signed and placed in the lawyer's vault for safe-keeping. The business prospered. The partners were hiring more and more office assistants and mortgage closers each year. Community Corners Mortgage was the top destination on the housing loan horizon. They advertised widely on television, on radio, and in all of the major newspapers in the Washington, D.C. corridor. Al and Sid had more money than they had ever dreamed possible.

Sid stood and looked out of the window of their spacious suite of offices on a gray, rainy day and scowled. He was in a predicament. From the day they met over ten years earlier, whenever he looked at Al, he felt a sensation that almost took his breath away. He had merged with Robbie because of this deep, gnawing hunger in his soul to have deep and authentic feelings and to experience wholeness. It had been somewhat effective. He had been able to please his parents and his business associates after that by pretending. First, by achieving perfection in his studies, and then by learning and mimicking mannerisms that made others think he was kind and compassionate. Actually, beneath the surface he felt rage and anger almost all the time. When it came to a rolling boil, he needed an outlet. In the case of Robbie, it had been the accident. With his boring parents, it had been the fire. He now felt almost a sexual attraction toward the personality of Al Fisher, though not toward the man himself. He resented the goodness and sincerity of his business partner and he wanted, no, he longed in a visceral way, to possess Albert Fisher's pure soul and spirit and to merge them in one violent paroxysm and spiritual orgasm with his deficient ones.

His fingers began to open and close. His hands clenched into fists, and his sexual organ throbbed with an intensity that made him want to cry out with pain and urgency. He mopped sweat from his brow and collapsed on the chocolate-colored leather couch in his office, waves of emotion coursing through his body. Tears came to his eyes, and he rubbed at them fiercely. He had to get a grip! He reached for a glass of water and drank it all in one gulp. It took a tremendous act of will to quiet his racing heart and calm himself. He would think rationally and calmly. He would find a way to meet this most urgent and increasingly vital goal.

"Carefully, carefully," he told himself. "The prize is so great. It is so close." Sid could almost taste the sweet and slightly salty taste of a transfusion of the pure innocence of Al's inner essence. He smiled his strange, distant smile, fought hard to focus his special, unique and powerful eye, and silently rejoiced.

Chapter Twenty

What is Love if Not a
Commodity to be Purchased

Sid, 1989

Within a few days after returning to Maryland from his parents' funeral in 1979, Sid had contacted the local county agency that screened youthful felony offenders and prepared them for their court hearings. He was welcomed and given a volunteer position based on his excellent record of service in New York State. The routine screening found him to be eminently qualified and a model citizen. He was assigned a cubicle in a busy office, and no one bothered him as he went about his duties interviewing young male felony offenders and following their progress through trial and imposition of sentence or release with or without probation.

He had become a valuable and trusted volunteer over the years and had expanded his theory about the young teenaged boys who were charged with felonies and incarcerated in prison starting at age 15. The crimes often consisted of stealing a car for a few hours to go joyriding, or stealing a few cartons of cigarettes and some beer from a gas station. Sometimes drugs were involved, but not usually with boys who lived in upstate rural areas. Those who were sentenced to prison terms, however, were often kept on various medications to keep them "calm" in prison. They served their sentences and then were unable to find employers who would hire them. They also might have become addicted to the medications they received in prison. Sid saw this as a colossal waste of taxpayer money. No one was benefitting. He looked for alternatives.

In 1989, Sid's partner, Albert Fisher, suddenly and unexpectedly died by committing suicide at a remote campsite in the mountains. Sid became the owner and director of their mortgage company and decided to make the move to Fairfax County in Virginia where a boom in housing was predicted. Commuters via the beltway to the District were clamoring for upscale housing. Sid seized the opportunity. He found an apartment in adjacent Prince William County, where the rents were still low, and was pleased to learn that he could purchase the penthouse suite, which occupied the entire top floor of a building, for what he considered to be a reasonable amount. He wanted to adapt to the finer things in life, as he believed this would increase his sensitivity in all areas.

It was about this time that he met one of the most inspiring people of his life. He was having a hamburger special with fries and coleslaw at a restaurant near the office. There were several men at the bar drinking beer and he overheard them discussing mortgage rates. One of them, who was strikingly handsome with wavy black hair, a muscular build, and piercing eyes, looked in Sid's direction and noticed him sitting there. He motioned Sid over. Sid reluctantly left the burger and went over and stood near them at the bar.

"Say, aren't you the new rising star and director of Community Corners Mortgage?" the man asked.

Sid mentally shuffled through his internal "Rolodex" of appropriate facial expressions and decided on a "sincere smile." "Yes," he said, looking directly at the speaker and putting on his version of a wide grin.

The man extended his hand, "Pull up a stool and join us," he said, "I'm Ross Barnes, this is Pete Wells, and on the end, that redhead is young Joe Bowen." They all nodded at each other. Sid felt an electric current spike through his body as

Barnes touched his hand. For a moment he was dizzy, but quickly recovered. He was used to being in control at all times!

Sid made an effort and was able to keep his gaze steady and his direct look intact. "I'm having a hamburger over there," he gestured to the booth. "Why don't you join *me*."

There was a pause as Barnes considered the offer. He was accustomed to having the upper hand, but he was curious about the bold younger man. "OK," he agreed finally. Nodding to the others he said, "Let's see what this kid has to say for himself." The two men got down from their stools and followed their leader to the booth.

Sid knew that the next move was crucial to the success of the plan. He had a wily sixth sense that alerted him that this was an auspicious meeting. He waited for Ross to speak. For a few minutes, the discussion of mortgage rates continued. They talked about the newly relaxed guideline for mortgage eligibility and the "adjustable rates" that were making it possible for even those with low income and questionable credit to be approved for new home loans. They were all so busy making money that they couldn't believe their good fortune. Cash was rolling in and they were enjoying record commissions. Ross was looking at Sid with interest as he spoke. Sid was not only knowledgeable, he was a smooth talker and had the charisma of a sales star.

Sid finished his hamburger and soft drink. The others finished their beers and got up to leave. Before Sid could join them, Ross whispered to him, "Hold on a minute. I'll be right back." For some reason, Sid felt that familiar excitement that sometimes came over him. He was having trouble breathing, so he just gave a quick nod. Ross walked outside with his friends, then came back and sat down across from Sid in the booth. He looked directly into his eyes and asked softly, almost purring like a jungle cat, "Tell me about yourself."

Sid's heart was racing. He felt the power of this man and wanted to be enveloped by it. He barely had the energy to pull out a small, somewhat friendly smile and put it on. "There's not much to tell," he answered. Ross gave him a look of genuine kindness. "Will you have a drink with me?" he asked. Sid made it a rule never to drink anything containing alcohol when discussing business. This was not business, though. It was two business men getting acquainted. They ordered two whiskeys and sat sipping them. Sid felt the warmth of the alcohol enter his system. The second drink gave him a pleasant little buzz. He was so relaxed and so grateful for this, the first authentic social interaction he had experienced with another human for so many years. Ross asked him again, in that soft, seductive voice that seemed to caress all of the sharp edges of Sid's personality and soften them, "Please tell me about yourself, Sid."

"I'm so lonely." The words slid out unbidden, and he immediately regretted his mistake. Ross gently took both of Sid's hands in his and whispered, "So am I. Will you take a walk with me so that we can talk more privately about it?" He rose from the bench and Sid followed. Sid was shaking from emotion and having trouble walking. Ross left money on the table and when they reached the door he opened it and Sid went out first. Out on the sidewalk they turned and looked at each other. Ross mouthed the words, "Thank you," and put his arm through Sid's as they walked. The connection was electric. Sid experienced waves of pleasure that were transmitted through Ross's light touch. All of the sensations that his body had experienced when he was in the presence of the young men at the probation office were magnified a hundred fold. He shivered with delight and a groan escaped his lips.

Ross stopped and put his arms around Sid. He pulled him into a tender embrace and stroked Sid's lips lightly with his finger. "It's your first time, isn't it?" he said. Sid couldn't speak, so he nodded.

Ross said in a hoarse whisper, "I want this to be special for you. Will you come to my place with me?" Sid would have gone to the bottom of the sea with this man if he had suggested it. He nodded, still not trusting himself to speak. "Did you drive or walk," Ross asked. "Walked." "OK, we'll take a cab." He hailed a taxi and gave the address. At the apartment building they entered a private elevator and rode to the penthouse. Ross smiled as he opened the door and turned to kiss Sid gently. Then he took him by the hand and led him into the bedroom. He asked him to sit on the king-sized bed and then proceeded to gently undress him, kissing and caressing each newly exposed area of skin as he worked. "Do the same for me, please darling," he said, taking Sid's hand and placing it on his erection. "Please undress me so that our bodies can touch as closely as possible." Sid pulled gently at Ross's clothing and removed his shirt and was working on his belt when he felt his own body explode in a giant orgasm. "Oh God, oh God, I'm so sorry," he cried out, shaking with the pleasure of it, but knowing it was too soon.

Ross pulled off his own trousers and pressed his body into Sid's. Sid's erection returned almost immediately. "Take me in your mouth," Ross panted. He pushed Sid into a position where he could do this, and showed him how to bring Ross to orgasm. After that, they lay laughing on the gigantic bed and Ross rumpled his hair. "So, what did you think of that, virgin boy?" he asked with a smile.

"I want to do it again!" They showered together and massaged each other's bodies. By the time the sun rose, Sid had fallen in love with sex. He had discovered the outlet for his stress and a temporary respite to his disdain for others. He was willing to give some attention to other men in order to reap the reward of that empowering total sexual release for himself.

He was impatient to get to the office the next morning, but he tolerated having breakfast and some conversation with Ross. As it turned out, it was a good thing he did. Ross laid out for him some profitable opportunities that they could share in the sex arena. Ross was a mortgage broker, but he lived in luxury. He had the penthouse apartment in a high-rise building in Fairfax County, Virginia. The apartment was the size of a house. It consisted of four bedrooms, four baths, a luxurious living room, a designer kitchen, and a formal dining room. There was also a fully equipped theater.

It was about the theater that Ross wished to speak. He showed a brief film clip to Sid. The film was of a boy of about 16 and a man of about 30 engaging in steamy sex. Both actors were physically fit and they moved in graceful, evocative motions, almost like an erotic dance. It was giving Sid another erection just watching them. Ross turned off the projector and explained that it was his hobby and a lucrative side business to give parties to bring together boys and men who would like to have a good time.

There was a charge for this entertainment and the boys had to be compensated for their services. This was how they made their living, as jobs for non-college graduates were scarce. To Sid's surprise, the meeting at the restaurant the day before had not been an accident. Ross knew that Sid frequently stopped there for a burger after work. He had thoroughly investigated Sid before their meeting and had also talked with his employers at his volunteer job in the county office.

One of the sources of "guests" at Ross's parties was the criminal-justice system. Young men who had committed criminal acts such as stealing cars or merchandise or writing bad checks were frequently not wanted at home and not able to find employment. They were willing workers in the sex industry. Referrals were made by lawyers working within Ross's network. There was a fee charged to the business men attending the parties of $1000 a night. The boys were paid room and board and received clothing and all the necessities for a life of luxury. Ross was willing to work with Sid on a commission basis if he would take part in recruiting young men who were either already out of jail and on the street, or eligible to be bailed out of jail. Ross added, "You can join my little group and be my partner in this work, and we can also enjoy some good times together just as we did last night. I'm looking to expand the business and make it much safer for us by setting up some permanent housing and a new system of recruitment."

He asked Sid to consider it and to meet him for dinner around 8:00 that night. "We can eat here, Sid," he said. "I'll have my chef come in and prepare a meal for us. He's very discreet. That way we can have some time alone together instead of eating in a crowded public place."

Sid's heart sang! He had already made a decision. This was what he had waited for so impatiently for the past 15 years. His dream was to be a reality!! There was to be financial insurance for his future, and it was miles beyond the utter boredom of his former life! He would say "Yes!" but not until he had the thrill of another night of electrifying sex.

Chapter Twenty-one
Passion and Pursuit

1995

The weeks, months, and years that followed were incredible to Sid. He had found the ultimate outlet for his power and passion. The merging experiences that accompanied naked, sweaty sex were beyond anything he had ever envisioned or imagined. He could strip off his clothes, take off the annoying hearing aids, and deliciously merge his body with that of another. It was a silent act in slow motion. He could hear nothing without the hearing aids, and that gave him pleasure. It heightened his sense of touch and taste and smell. It was an urgent, feral act. His powerful eye could observe every fluid motion of his body and that of whomever his partner was on a given day or evening. He was becoming a new person. A power unto himself.

As time went by, Sid and Ross became more skilled in recruiting teenage boys for the "club." The cover name was "The Planning Committee." By the early-1990s, they had expanded the business way beyond what Ross had ever imagined. They found that there was, among these outcasts from society, a hunger to belong, to be a part of something. The young boys who had been rejected by the mainstream were thrilled to be members of a fraternal organization and to be living a life of ease at the same time.

They only recruited boys without parents or responsible adults in their lives. Actually, the club membership and working for room and board kept them off the street. Sometimes boys would be in danger of a prison sentence, but if a responsible adult came forward and offered a job, the court would release them to that person. This was an easy transition. Sid had direct access to the files that contained the records of the boys' past, including their family histories. It was easy for him to slip pages out of the files and take them home to share with Ross, so that they could choose the teens who would best suit their purposes.

They decided that the young men they recruited should be carefully controlled to ensure the utmost secrecy and safety for their lucrative operation. Ross suggested that with the increasing volume of business, the system of paying the boys a cash stipend was not secure enough. Ross and Sid came up with a much more sophisticated approach. There was an almost unlimited market for the services of their "recruits" among the wealthy businessmen who were pouring into the area. The recruits had to be contained in a carefully controlled situation. They also had to be isolated from all outside influences.

Ross and Sid expanded their purchase of exclusive properties that contained luxury one-bedroom apartments. They conceived of the idea of placing one teenaged boy in each apartment with a staff of two people who would clean and prepare meals. The boys would be lured into the situation as an alternative to jail by being told they were being "hired" as actors. They would live in luxury with just one responsibility: to be available 24 hours a day to perform sexual acts requested by "guests." Usually there would be only one guest during any 24-hour period. The sessions would vary in length, usually no more than two or three hours at a time. The teens would receive abundant food, room and board, clothing, and video games. They would be taken to exercise in the building's exercise room for an hour each day, but would not leave the building. Each apartment would have a state-of-the-art theater where video games and movies could be accessed as well as special "erotic" films that the boy and his guests could enjoy together.

One of the boys who had been close to going to prison in 1994 after committing a series of petty thefts was a boy named Jeremy. Jeremy was clean-cut and good looking. Sid had stepped forward, on impulse, and volunteered to sponsor him. Jeremy had no living parents or other relatives. Sid paid the lawyer who helped them with "challenges" that arose during recruiting members of the Club to prepare convincing documents stating that he, Sid, was Jeremy's uncle. The court released the boy to Sid without any probation supervision.

Sid was in love with sex, and he briefly enjoyed the challenge of teaching Jeremy to understand the process. However, he had no emotional attachment to Jeremy. To him, the boy was just another scientific experiment, much as he had been to his own adoptive parents, Una and David. Sid taught Jeremy how sexual arousal feels and how to entice another man to perform sex acts. The problem was that Jeremy, unlike Ross, wanted to experience "love." That was out of the question for Sid. He had a love of power, a love of money, and a love of sexual stimulation. He had no interest in or idea of the love that people talked about that involved friendship and caring.

Occasionally, Sid had fleeting thoughts of what it might be like to really care about someone, but he quickly dismissed such thoughts as signs of character weakness. His focus had always been to nurture the strengths that led to his power over others. Robbie and Al had shown themselves to have pure souls. He had removed that aspect from them and merged with it to give his soul the characteristic that it lacked, but in Sid's case nothing was exhibited except the power to impress and to feign purity of soul and spirit. He could only "act as if" he was kind and generous and lure anyone into trusting and obeying his every wish and desire. To Sid, that was sufficient.

Sid had moved Jeremy into Sid's apartment. This had been a mistake, Sid decided almost immediately. Sid did not want to spend time with Jeremy. He wanted to be making the rounds of the apartments where the teenage boys were always ready to perform their prescribed roles and to accommodate his sexual desires. He also wanted to be with Ross, who had the advantage of years of sexual experience.

Sid got into a routine of dropping off Jeremy at the private school in the morning, picking him up after classes were over for the day, and dropping him at the apartment. Then he would immediately turn the car around and go out to the apartments or to Ross's place for the night. He would return home in time to drive Jeremy to school the next morning. He was getting the urge to be with these random sexual partners more often. Sometimes mid-afternoon the desire would be so strong that he had to feed it like an addiction. He was able to control this to some extent, but at least once a month he had to satisfy the increasingly intense craving and go to one of the Planning Committee locations right away.

At these times, he would call an architect named Jess Sampson, a very dull, ordinary, uninteresting person who would never suspect that anything was wrong. Jess had brought in a number of customers for mortgages in connection with Jess's housing construction company. Jess was 100% reliable, though unimaginative. This made Jess perfect for playing the role of an honorary relative to young Jeremy. Boring Jess would become known as "Uncle Jess," and he would never suspect anything.

Moving Jeremy into his house had been wrong. It was a mistake that he would not make again. Gradually, Sid was becoming obsessed with trying to correct the "mistake", no matter what it took.

Chapter Twenty-two
Inside Story of Successful Recruitment

There arose, in the 1980s, seemingly out of nowhere, a group known as The Planning Committee, which purchased or leased a number of luxury apartments throughout the Washington D.C. corridor. Their territory extended into Virginia to the south and Maryland to the north. The organization neither owned nor leased property in its own name, but in the names of a myriad of corporate entities set up as limited liability corporations through the liberal licensing laws of the state of Delaware. Its existence was a closely guarded secret for many years.

The structure was developed to provide cover for a web of operatives in the human trafficking of young adolescent boys. Members, who were exclusively male, were issued code names and given instructions on how to maintain secure phone lines and internet connections. Their source of supply was established through connections within the correctional facilities and the probation offices throughout the area.

The plan was to put young juvenile offenders "in jobs" to avoid the economic burden of incarceration.

What follows are a few example of the "stories" of some of the young men who were recruited by and who quickly disappeared into the intricate web of the Planning Committee. Their stories, using fictitious names, were recorded by Executive Director Ross Barnes to serve as part of a portfolio to whet the sexual appetites of new and existing members with actual examples of what was available to them. Barnes also wanted members of The Committee to understand the valuable service they were performing for the community by taking these "delinquents" off the streets and "rehabilitating" them.

Some might have disagreed with this approach to rehabilitation and would have seen it as an Rx for Recidivism. Ross and Sid would have just smiled knowingly at such a "short sighted" view of their work. Because the recruits did not survive their teen age years, the project was not at all a prescription for recidivism. It came, instead, with an absolute guarantee of satisfactory completion of the program and the 100% successful eradication of the young person's criminal tendencies.

Alan (as recorded by Ross Barnes)

"When I was 15, right after I'd been sentenced to probation in court for taking cigarettes and stuff from the gas station, I was hanging out with some kids. We were skipping school and one of them, named Joe, asked if I would like to go swimming after lunch. I told him I knew of a place to swim. So after lunch we rode our bicycles out to the creek on Sawyer Road. We left our bikes in the bushes just off the road and went down the hill to the creek. After we were there for a few minutes Joe and I decided that I would go down the road a way to see if Dan Miller would like to swim with us. Dan wasn't home, so I went back to the creek. I was wearing my red swimming trunks with a white stripe. We swam for a few minutes. I looked up and saw a man standing at the edge of the road looking down at us. He looked like he was about 20 or 30 years old and was a couple inches taller than me. He had black hair that was combed back and he was wearing a white T shirt and gray pants.

"We were building a little dam of stones to hold the water back. The man called down and asked us how the water was. I

said, 'It's cold!' Joe and I then walked to the culvert that went under the road to get some more stones for the dam. We climbed up the culvert onto the road with some of the stones and we began throwing them down into the water from the other side of the road.

The man was a few feet from us by then. He said, 'If this water was a little deeper I'd like to dive into it!' I said, 'Last year my friend used to jump into the water from the culvert.'

"*The man then walked around in back of me and put his arms around me. He put his right hand on my chest just under my throat and his left hand on my swimming trunks over my private parts. I was scared, but I didn't struggle. He asked me how old I was, and I told him 15. Then he asked, 'Do you have any hair?' He didn't say where, but I knew what he meant. I said, 'Yes.'*

"*'Would you show me?'*"

"*I said, 'No.'*"

"*He asked, 'Do you want a blow job?'*"

"*I said, 'No!'*"

"*Meanwhile, Joe was walking backward a few steps at a time to try to reach the nearest house to ask to use the phone to call for help.*

"*The man rubbed my private parts and then let go of me and stood in front of me. He kept asking me to please show him and asking why I wouldn't. We were on the shoulder of the road all this time. He asked if I would go with him to a barn that was a short distance away where we could be alone. I said, 'NO!'*

"*I tried to walk away from the man, but he kept following me. He asked me, 'Did you ever do it to a girl?'*" I said, "No." "*I tried to walk away from him, but he grabbed me around the waist and tried to pull down my swimming trunks. I fell down, sitting on the ground. 'You <u>have</u> got hair,' he said. I was* *feeling excited now. I couldn't help it. I started wanting him to touch me again.*

"The man could see this. He stood a few feet away and didn't touch me anymore. He asked me if I was in school. I told him that I skipped school as much as I could. 'What do your parents say about that?' '"They don't say much,' I said. 'My old man is in prison and the old lady is drunk all the time and out on dates.'

"The man smiled. 'How would you like a job,' he asked?

"I called to Joe and told him everything was OK. He came over, looking scared. 'Let's go home,' he said. '

"You go on,' I told him. 'I've got to talk to this man about a job. I'll see you later.'" I jumped into the front seat of the car beside the man, waved to Joe, and off we went, leaving Joe behind. standing there with his mouth wide open.

"That was the start of my 'job' at the place called The Planning Committee. I got a new name, 'Alan.' I never went back home, and I'm sure I wasn't missed."

Chapter Twenty-three
Lure of the Silken Trap

Alan was his new name. It was explained that this was a sort of stage name and that every evening he would be "on stage." That was the job. He would be an actor. Alan was an innocent looking teen with a round face and dark brown eyes and wavy hair. He was of medium height and looked as if he hadn't had a good meal for weeks. He walked into the apartment where he would be living and working and literally gasped at what he saw.

Each of the business and professional men who were members of the club reserved a suitable apartment for themselves for each appointment, from the pool of choices, for their fantasies. There was a wide selection. The one that Alan was to occupy was a 2000 Square-Foot, one bedroom, two-bath luxury suite with lush pile carpet, a state of the art kitchen, a separate "rainforest" shower and a Jacuzzi in each bathroom, and two luxurious king-sized beds in the bedroom. The walls were done in muted pastels and there was a superb sound system that played a wide selection of music at the touch of a button.

Alan decided that this was Heaven. The job description was simple. He was to be a very close friend to whatever man came to the apartment each time (usually at night). The men, it was explained, were lonely and wanted to be loved. Alan wanted more than anything else to be loved too, so this he could understand. The men would let him know how that love was to be given, and it was up to him to perform as an actor and give them everything they most wanted to see, to feel, to experience.

The pay for the work was amazing. Alan was given a whole closet of work clothes. There were robes and revealing swim trunks as well as bikini underwear. Some of the men would want to see him in women's clothes, so there were some of those, too. Some of them would want him to pretend to be their son and to dress up in a suit and tie. Whatever they wanted, there was a costume that would fit the part. Meals were included, and employees had a choice of excellent meals served to them by the household staff. Cleaning and laundry were part of the package.

The most amazing room of all was the Home Theater. It was a room equipped with projectors and screens and state of the art stereo. The TVs had large screens and were of various sizes. Soft leather couches and chairs were positioned around the room at points where access to the screens was the most advantageous. There was a large library of erotic films to get the men in the mood to fondle and to engage in a wide variety of sexual acts with the boys. Part of the training was for the boys to watch these films and learn the skills they would need to practice if they were to please the clients.

There was no leaving the job or quitting. Once a boy was hired, it was for an indeterminate period of time to be decided only by the employer. Alan wondered if he would ever be considered to be too old to be appealing to the clients. He quickly put that idea out of his mind and concentrated on doing his best to fulfill his role.

The men who reserved the various apartments paid between $2000 an hour and $10,000 per 24 hour day for the privilege. The boys were not paid in cash, but in room, board and clothing. They were supervised by the household staff in each living unit who made sure they never had access to the exit code that would let them get off the elevator on the ground floor and leave the building. They had no access to telephones or to online computer accounts. They were allowed to live in Paradise, but they were never to leave. This was OK with him.

Alan never saw any other boys while he was employed by the syndicate that operated The Planning Committee. He had no idea if there were others like himself who were captives in this strange world. He was grateful in a way that his life was so closely regulated. He didn't have to go to school. He enjoyed the work and loved the attention being paid to his body. He didn't have to worry about how to make money because he had everything he needed. He didn't have to even think about going to jail, because he was living a magical life in which stealing wasn't necessary. He could watch all the TV he wanted to in his off-duty hours. He could choose from a full library of video games.

The clients were allowed to use drugs and alcohol, but the boys were forbidden to consume any alcohol or illegal drugs or to smoke. The staff closely monitored this and served the clients their substances of choice, which of course the clients paid for. Cocaine was the most popular. The men said it helped them relax and made their minds sharper at the same time.

Some clients wanted to drink until they were unable to stand, which was fine with Alan. All he had to do was to throw a blanket over the man when he passed out and let him sleep it off until the next morning.

Chapter Twenty-four
Case Studies of Recruits

Ray (as recorded by Ross Barnes)

"I was staying part of the time with my aunt at her house and sometimes with my friend, Keith out in the country. On April 14, I was in the City Grill from about midnight to 1 AM. When I left, I walked for a couple blocks and saw a Thunderbird parked at a gas station. I went over to the car and saw the keys were in the ignition. I got in the car and started it up and drove away. I drove for about an hour and then I saw that a state trooper was following me with his flashing light on. I didn't want to be stopped so I gunned the engine and drove as fast as I could. The state trooper kept following me, but the Thunderbird went into a little ditch and stopped. The trooper that was chasing me came over and arrested me.

"I didn't have anyone to bail me out, so I went to jail that night. The next morning a man came to the jail to see me and said he knew a lawyer who would help me. He asked me my age, and I told him 16. The lawyer had sent this man with bail money. I got out and he took me to the lawyer's house. The lawyer told me to call him 'Bob.' He let me shower and gave me some clean clothes. While I was in the shower he came in the bathroom without any clothes on and asked me if he could get in the shower with me. I was a little scared, but I said 'Sure' because I wanted him to help me. He had some oil that he rubbed all over me after the shower. It felt good, and I got less scared. And then he did other things that felt good. After he helped me dress, we had breakfast and he asked me if I would like to stay in one of his apartments in the District. He

said he would give me a job and pay all my expenses. I thought it was too good to be true, but when we went there, I saw it was the best break I ever had. All I had to do was to let the men that came there fool around with me. All my expenses would be paid and I could watch TV when I was there alone and eat great food. I got a new name. It was Ray."

Chris (as recorded by Ross Barnes)

"One Sunday I came to Rockville with my friend, John. My friend let me out and went on to his job somewhere in southern Virginia. I went to several bars. I was feeling pretty good. Then I walked to the college and noticed one of the windows was unlocked. I ripped the screen off the window and opened the window and climbed in. After climbing in, I bought a candy bar from the vending machine, tore all the papers off the bulletin board, and took a leak in the women's room. I opened the window in the women's room and climbed up and jumped outside. I saw a truck out there. The keys were in the ignition. I got into the truck and started it up and drove it away from the college. I thought I was driving toward the District but actually I was driving the other way. About 10 miles up the road I went off on the shoulder and the truck rolled over on its top. I crawled out and started walking down the road, and a man in a Chevy that was passing by picked me up. We saw the flashing lights of a state police car coming toward us as we drove along. I asked him to drop me at the state police, and he did. I told them that I was the one who robbed the Ford truck from the college and crashed it. They took me to jail. The next morning, I went to court to be arraigned. There was to be no bail.

"A man in the courtroom came up to talk to the judge. After that, I was released to this man. He asked me how old I was and I told him 17. He asked me who I lived with, and I told him I live on

my own and I have no contact with my parents. My mother and stepfather live somewhere in Brooklyn. I lived out in the country in Maryland with some friends.

We went to a diner and had a good breakfast, and the man, whose name was Bert, asked me if I would like a job. I said, 'Sure.' We went to his house which was like a mansion. He took my hand and we went upstairs to his bedroom. I was a little scared, but he was really nice and he showed me all of the upstairs rooms and his TV. He asked me if I would watch a movie with him. He said it would be fun if we watched it with no clothes on. We took off our clothes and he took my hand again and we went into his bathroom and he put warm water in the Jacuzzi and we sat in it and he kissed me and rubbed me all over with soap. It was like nothing I ever felt before. I didn't want him to stop. Then we sat on the couch wrapped up in a giant bath towel together and watched a movie about a guy my age and an older man getting it on together. I never saw anything like that. All the time we were watching it, Bert was touching me and I never wanted it to stop.

"After we laid on his bed for a while doing more of the same, he asked if I would like to go and see where the job would be that he was hoping I would take. We went in his car and drove south into Virginia. The apartment was huge, and I couldn't believe that it was for me. There are servants and everything. He told me what I would be doing and I was so glad that I had robbed that truck and gotten into court. All my expenses are paid and all I have to do is to let some quirky men pretend I'm their lover. I have a new name. It's Chris."

Chapter Twenty-five
Rehabilitation Reinterpreted

The project became the center of Sid's secret life, this business that was his dangerous and seductive hobby. He was addicted to visiting the apartments and sampling the delicacies of sex with the young boys. His desire was accelerating at a rapid pace. It had been almost a year since he had taken Jeremy in after Jeremy was released by the court from any requirement for probation. It had been his plan to adopt Jeremy and then to have him as his exclusive sexual partner. Somehow this plan had been derailed almost immediately.

The problem was that Jeremy was so polite, so kind, so trusting, so smart in school, so competent, that Sid began to hate and resent him almost at once. Jeremy was making Sid look inferior, Sid warned himself. He had no desire to merge with Jeremy. Robbie and Al had been weak and vulnerable. Jeremy was the opposite of that. He was pure of heart, but he would be a mighty force within Sid and would destroy him with that strength. In fact, Jess and Jeremy were both do-gooders who were making Sid look weak by comparison.

Being with Ross Barnes had changed everything. Sid's desire not only for their "employees" but also for Ross was almost insatiable. He had gone into partnership with Ross and had provided many leads in the recruiting process. He had become expert many years before in slipping copies of files from the probation records and passing their contents on to the recruiters. They now had a steady supply of teenaged boys as well as businessmen who would pay almost anything for assignations with them. The business was so lucrative that he and Ross had a number of offshore accounts in which to conceal the money.

When Ross had first started the business there had been a major problem with addiction among the boys. They were either living on the streets or in dysfunctional families. Many were using cocaine, alcohol, or heroin. The new system had corrected all of that and had made the business much safer and much more lucrative. The system of buying luxury living quarters, staffing them, and charging much higher fees had made the difference. There was only one teenager per living unit. That way, there was complete control over the boys and a much expanded revenue stream from the club members who felt safer when they themselves were the only drug users. There were, however, special situations where a member would request the services of more than one boy at a time. These were handled on an individual basis.

The general rule was that each boy would be isolated from any of the others. Each would be confined to his own living quarters at all times. Everything would be brought to them.

Sid and Ross were aware that the "shelf life" of each of their recruits was limited. They would only be teens for a few years. Once a boy reached a certain age where he was no longer marketable, they had planned an "exit strategy" whereby the boy was taken to a heavily wooded area owned by Ross and eliminated. The youngster was buried deeply so that no animal would be tempted to dig him up. This was part of the business plan and was treated in a matter of fact manner by both Ross and Sid. They were not dependent on any of the recruits. There were always many more where they had come from. And, they reasoned, it was saving the local government the cost of incarcerating "young punks."

Sid was feeling very unsettled about Jeremy. He was worried that he was arousing suspicion in that dull Jess

Harkness by continuing to ask him to transport Jeremy from school to home. Even someone as unimaginative as Jess would eventually catch on that all was not well. He made a decision to get rid of Jeremy and to include Jess in the plan. It would be simple. He would get them out to the campground and finish them off there.

In spite of his great success, Sid brooded over his own foolishness in taking in Jeremy. He couldn't take any more chances. Just the other night Jeremy had gotten bored and had walked down to Sid's satellite office near the apartment to meet him and had unexpectedly caught him giving Ross Barnes a passionate goodnight kiss. The kid had no right to spy on him like that and to ruin his life. Yes, Jeremy had to go. And now!

Chapter Twenty-six
Camping

So far, all Jess knew was that Jeremy seemed like a normal high school student and that Sid somehow trusted Jess, and no one else, to reliably and consistently transport Jeremy from school to his home. Jess felt increasingly uneasy about Jeremy's safety, and found himself, as he often did, consulting the spiritual energy he knew as Allison about it. He definitely felt encouragement coming from Allison as to his doing something proactive to help Jeremy. He decided to be more vigilant, to be very cautious around Sid, and to watch closely for any signals of impending trouble from Jeremy.

He was also getting messages he knew were from Allison that he should be taking on assistants in his business so that he could be freed up to travel if necessary. He didn't understand this, but he followed his intuition. He trusted that his greatest security and success would come if he surrendered to what he believed. Through the summer and fall of 1996 he took on a full staff of associates and cross-trained them in every aspect of the business.

Sid eventually began to refer to Jess as "Uncle Jess." Jeremy picked it up, and over the next few months Jess found himself not only accepting but enjoying the role.

After Thanksgiving with his parents in Florida, Jess returned to Virginia intent on discovering more about the relationship between Jeremy and Sid.

One day, in the second week of December, during a period of unusually warm winter weather, he received a call from Sid asking for a very different favor. Sid asked Jess to pick up Jeremy at noon on a Friday when there would be early dismissal and drive him to a camping site in the wooded hills of Maryland. Sid said that he wanted to start out at daybreak to set up the camp. If Jeremy could join him early in the afternoon they would have a fun weekend together doing some tracking and hunting, sleeping in one of the cabins, and cooking over a campfire.

Jess felt some sort of warning bell go off in his mind, but he did not dare to suggest any such thing to Sid. Once again, he followed his intuition and simply agreed. The directions would take them to an old logging road where they would park Jess's car and walk to the campsite. When he stopped at the school for Jeremy, he saw that the boy had a backpack, which he assumed contained his camping gear. This was the last day of class before winter break. There would be no more school until mid-January. Jeremy did not seem excited to be going camping. In fact, after saying hello to Jess, he was silent for the entire trip. Jess turned on the radio and listened to a talk show to try to put the boy at ease. They walked quietly just a few feet from the car, toward the trail. Almost at once, Jeremy stopped abruptly and sat down.

PART III

JEREMY

Chapter Twenty-seven
Jeremy Speaks

The handsome lanky teenager with the slight build, tousled blonde hair, and blazing blue eyes sank down on a log, put his head in his hands, and began to sob uncontrollably.

"What's all this about?" Jess asked, uncomfortable with the torrent of tears and not used to dealing with teenagers in any mood.

"I'm in trouble," the boy gasped between sobs. He looked so vulnerable, so wounded. The big man started to move toward him uncertainly.

"Don't come any closer!" the boy said in a soft, menacing voice, so unlike his usual shy manner. "Touch me, and I'll kill you, I swear!" His face contorted, he looked so wounded and so out of control that Jess stepped back abruptly and sat down on a small spot of grass a few feet from the log.

"I hate camping! I don't want to go any farther!" The sobs began again with even more intensity.

"Do you want to tell me about it?" Jess asked quietly. "Maybe I can help. Jeremy, I really mean it. I want to help you if I can."

Jeremy lowered his head and wiped the sleeve of his denim jacket across his nose and cheeks. "I don't know," he said so softly that it was almost inaudible, "I guess it can't get any worse! For starters, Sid isn't really my uncle."

Jess nodded encouragement, and Jeremy went on.

"Somehow he got the court to believe that he was my uncle when he bailed me out, after I got busted for taking the candy and beer and cigarettes from the gas station. He took me home with him."

"He gave you a home?"

"Yeah. At first he was good to me. He treated me like a son, I guess. In those first weeks he bought me clothes and CDs and all the food I wanted. Then he began to tell me he wanted us to be closer than that. He said he was falling in love with me. He asked me if I'd ever been in love with a boy, and I said, "No, I thought that was something boys and girls did. I had a girlfriend a couple times, but we weren't in love."

Jeremy took a long, ragged breath and then continued, "Sid said he wanted me to learn to feel real adult love, so he would sit next to me on the couch while we watched movies on TV about men in love. He would put his arms around me and stroke my hair. It felt so good – I wanted to get even closer to him. Soon we were kissing, and it was a wonderful feeling. It was the most exciting thing that had ever happened in my life! He began to stroke me all over my body! I felt like I was in Heaven. It took away all the memories of the pain of beatings from my old man and the screaming of my old lady. It made me feel clean and beautiful. We were so much in love!"

The crying began again, softly this time, as Jeremy remembered those early days of his relationship with his mentor.

Jeremy continued, "We began to lie on Sid's bed together. We played a game of kissing and rubbing against each other and taking off some clothes each time we kissed until we were naked and lying in each other's arms hugging, kissing, stroking…."

Jess interrupted, alarmed at the way the conversation was going. "God, Jeremy, you're only 16 years old! I had no idea that was going on!"

Jeremy's eyes filled with tears again. "Jess, the trouble is that I'm crazy in love with him, but I'm so afraid there's someone else and I'm going to lose him. I think he asked me on this camping trip because I found out he's been seeing a guy from work at the bank. I wasn't supposed to know. He told me that he had to work late Tuesday night but that he'd be home after that. I went home after school, but I missed him so much that I decided to walk down to the bank where he said he had a closing, and wait for him to come out so we could walk home together. When I got there, I saw him and this other guy coming out the door. I hid around the side of a pillar and watched them go down the steps holding hands and laughing.

"When they got to the street, they kissed really deeply and then the other man walked off in the opposite direction, and Sid started toward where I was standing. I didn't know what to do, I just ran over and blurted out, 'What were you doing?!'

"Sid looked like a deer in the headlights and then he said, 'We went to dinner and worked on some stuff in the office, and then I kissed him goodnight.'

"Sid ruffled my hair like nothing was wrong and leaned close to me, 'You know I'm a passionate guy, and you know that you're Number One with me!'

"He threw his arms around me right there on the sidewalk and gave me a soft, slow kiss. I could smell that piney aftershave of his, and my body just caved into his as it always does. 'Let's go home and make love,' he whispered while he gently kissed my ear. Another kiss with his tongue wrapping around mine, and his beard stubble gently brushing against my cheek, and my whole body was shaking and exploding against his.

"I couldn't wait to make love to him in our bed. It was the best ever. Later, he fed me French vanilla ice cream with his finger, and we made love again slowly and in perfect rhythm. We were so close at that moment I thought we could never be apart again."

"When did the subject of the camping trip come up?" Jess asked.

Jeremy continued, "We woke up the next morning and just lay there kissing and smiling until it was time for me to go to school and for him to go to work. Sid had been staying out all night working for months, but he told me that project was finished and we would be together every night from then on. Sid told me about the surprise he had for us to get away for the whole weekend for a camping trip in his favorite woods. He said he had to come up here early on Friday morning to get the campsite ready. He said, 'Don't worry. I've asked Uncle Jess to pick you up after school ends on Friday afternoon. He'll take you to the campsite, and we'll cook dinner together in the woods and stay in the cabin.'

"Uncle Jess, I'm so afraid I'm going to lose him. I don't know what to do. If I lose Sid, I don't want to live anymore."

Jess sat bolt upright and looked directly at the boy. "Jeremy, you're 16. Sid's a grown man of 40. You know so little about him. From what you're telling me, he sure is taking advantage of your trust in him. Let me think a minute before we get back on the trail."

Jess often wondered in later years what would have happened if he had listened to the "voice of reason" in his head that advised him to move forward on the trail and confront Sid directly to try to salvage young Jeremy's life before the boy's fantasy got completely out of hand. But there was another, insistent voice that sensed great life-threatening danger if they moved forward even one more step in Sid's direction. The whole thing was strange. Why was Sid suddenly taking Jeremy, who had never been camping, deep into the forest, and why was he involving honorary "Uncle Jess?"

Jess knew little about Sid except for what he'd seen from contacts with him in business. And then, of course, there was that newspaper article that had mentioned the mysterious "suicide" of Sid's business partner. Sid sometimes seemed to be a friendly, outgoing man who some said was a great companion for a group that was going hunting or fishing, but he had never known him on a personal level. He had heard rumors of times when Sid was feared as a dangerous, out-of-control person. Jess had never seen that side of him. He had become "Uncle Jess" because of the many times he had picked Jeremy up from school or from his after-school job when Sid was allegedly out of town on business. His role had consisted of seeing that the boy had dinner and then dropping him off at Sid's apartment. Sid was rumored to be an expert fisherman and hunter, well-versed in survival skills in the forest. Yet, Sid had never included Jeremy in any of his alleged outdoor adventures. Something just didn't add up here.

There were very few minutes left in which to make a decision that would impact both of their lives forever. Jess looked around quickly. The oaks and maples had lost their leaves and offered no cover. But the branches of the pines, which would increase in number on the hike up the ridge to the campsite, were thick and lush and would conceal their presence if they made the climb. For that moment, Jess hesitated and weighed his choices. Was his imagination blowing this out of proportion? Maybe Sid had mellowed over the years and had lost any remaining aspects of the rumored "dark side." No, he couldn't take a chance. Jess pulled something out of his pocket and looked at Jeremy hesitantly.

"Look, Jeremy, I'm going to ask you to trust me in a big way on this. But in case you change your mind at any time, here's enough money to get you back here from wherever we end up today." With that he moved slightly forward and pushed $300.00 in twenties into Jeremy's hand. Jeremy stuffed the bills into his pocket and then looked in the direction of the trail to the camp as if he was considering running in that direction.

The next thing that happened was completely out of character for Jess, who liked to look carefully at all aspects of a problem and make a careful, reasoned decision before taking any action. He suddenly felt himself swerve mentally into "flight or fight" mode. There would be no discussion at this time, there could not be a murmur, let alone a yell or any sound of protest that would echo through the forest. He would have to act suddenly and assertively, catch Jeremy completely off guard, and apologize later. They had to get out of there immediately. Instinctively, he knew they were running for their lives.

After the decision was made, he did not hesitate a moment. Jess reached down and picked a startled Jeremy up in one smooth motion, threw him gently over his shoulder, holding him in a firm grip and began to run back the few feet back toward the SUV.

The suddenness of the action had the desired effect. Jeremy let out one gasp and then, miraculously, was silent. It was as if his heart and his mind held conflicting opinions and were stunned into silence. The forest was so still that it seemed that the birds and insects and other inhabitants had paused in their concert and were momentarily holding their breath.

A snake slithered silently across the path ahead of them. Jess nimbly jumped over it, not missing a step, and kept running as effortlessly as if he had trained for this. At the SUV, he deposited Jeremy in the passenger seat and buckled his seatbelt in one smooth motion. He put on the safety lock. As the engine started, Jeremy finally found his voice and shouted, "What the Fuck are you doing?! This is crazy, and you won't get away with kidnaping me!"

"Look kid . . . uh, Jeremy, there are things you don't understand. I can't talk about a lot of it right now, but I can ask you to trust me when I say that I may be saving your life. When we're safely away you'll know the details. Just try to believe this one thing. I know more about Sid than you do, and there are secrets in his life that he hasn't told either of us. So I hope you can trust me just enough to take you to a safe place where you can make your own decision about whether to go back."

Jeremy felt like he was going to throw up. He was so confused. An hour ago he had been dreading the camping trip, but the hope of being with his lover had kept him going. Still, how could he be sure of anything? Something had made him break down and tell everything to Jess. Jeremy had lived with parents who drank heavily, shouted and argued all the time, beat their son black and blue, and then passed out every day. His mother had sent his father away, and the beatings stopped. Her health was ruined by then, and though she tried to care for him, she spent the last months of her life as an invalid while he cared for her. His trust level of adults was not high. He had seen Sid hugging and kissing another man. Was the camping trip where Sid had promised they would be together in nature – just the two of them – for real - or was it a trap leading to some unknown danger? He had the $300 and decided to trust Jess for now.

Jess drove to his home in Montclair, grateful for the clear weather and the traffic-free highway. He parked in the garage, told Jeremy he would be right back, and ran into the house. Jeremy sat in the car and thought about opening the door and running … but running where? He was being asked by Jess to "trust." Trust had not served Jeremy well in the past. He had trusted his friends when they taught him to steal from small businesses. This had gotten him arrested. He had considered it an undeserved break when he had suddenly been released from jail and sent with Sid to a luxury apartment where he miraculously had adequate food and clothing. He had recently begun to realize that this had not been "freedom." He had been lured once again into trusting another person who had let him down.

The thought suddenly flashed through his mind that in this idyllic romance he had imagined, he had left out some essential details. Sid had, for many months, left him alone in the apartment all night every night while Sid was … where? He had no idea. He must have slept somewhere. His mind whirled again. Would "trusting" be any different with Jess? Here he sat with $300 in his pocket given to him by the one adult, other than his deceased mother in her last months of life, who had been dependable, kind, and caring and who had never, until today, asked him for anything in return. Yes, he was being asked to "trust." At this point, Jeremy was too confused and too emotionally exhausted to resist. He waited in the car and tried to quiet the turmoil in his mind.

Jess came back out, in only a few minutes, with three suitcases and a briefcase. They drove out onto the interstate, and Jess used a Motorola cell phone to call someone. Half an hour later they pulled up to a darkened building, and Jess turned off the engine. "We have to talk, Jeremy." Jeremy was scared and confused. He answered in a very small, shaky voice, "OK, Uncle Jess."

Jess said, "I had to make some fast decisions. I hope I didn't scare you too much! I wish we had a couple days to talk all this over and plan something we could agree on, but again, I have to ask you to trust for now and accept that there's danger involved and we have no choice but to try to put as much distance as possible between Sid and us. I am convinced Sid is not just a troubled man but is very mixed up and very dangerous. I have heard that in the past he killed very deliberately and systematically when he was out of control. He was clever and was never caught. I didn't know whether to believe this when I heard it, but I heard it more than once and based on what you told me today, I have to believe it could be true. When Sid asked me to pick you up after work and take you out there, I had planned to stay with the two of you just in case. . .

"Jeremy, do you have a juvenile record?"

"It was sealed because of my age. It was just petit larceny because it was the first time I was caught. Some of us busted into a couple gas stations a few times and took some gum and beer and cigarettes."

"OK, the record is sealed but they have your prints. We'll have to work on that. Are you on probation?"

"No. Sid told me that he made sure of that. He said he had a way of changing what was in the files and was able to lose files, too. Where are we going now?"

"We're going to buy a car from a friend of mine and get a passport for you."

Chapter Twenty-eight
Escape Route

Jeremy was silent as he took this in. They started driving again, and Jeremy suddenly felt himself unable to battle the confusion and conflicting emotions any longer. Exhausted and confused, he fell asleep. A few hours later, Jess pulled up to the gate of a sprawling ranch. He punched some numbers on the keypad, and the gate swung open. About two miles from the gate was a large house with white pillars and a lush, rolling lawn. Borders of flowers and neatly trimmed flowering hedges gave it an inviting look. A large dog bounded forward to greet them.

"Hey there, Barry," Jess called out as he climbed out of the car and rubbed the dog behind the ears, "it's good to see you again!" The dog looked to be smiling as he wagged his tail rapidly and then ran happily in circles around Jess.

A man in a navy-blue sweatshirt and jeans came out of the house and loped over to Jess in much the same way as had Barry. "Good to see you, man," he called out. "Likewise," Jess answered. "Jeremy, come on out of the car and meet my friend."

As Jeremy climbed out of the car, Jess's friend called out to him with a broad smile, "Wait here a minute, son, and get acquainted with Barry. We'll be right back." Barry and Jeremy tumbled around the lawn for a few minutes and Jeremy couldn't help but feel better. Jess came back shortly, driving a gray Subaru Forester that was a bit mud splashed. "We'll need to go into the house for a few minutes to get the ID," he said to Jeremy.

They sat in an office on the first floor while the stranger photographed Jeremy and applied something that smelled faintly like pineapple to his fingers to slightly alter his prints. He gave Jess one of the new mobile phones, a couple file folders and what looked like possibly a packet of tickets. Everything moved very fast and in silence.

Jess's friend had the connections to provide a place of safety for Jeremy and Jess. He had located a last-minute cancellation and had booked passage for them on a luxury cruise ship that was leaving on a world cruise the following day. This would provide safe passage and an appropriate cover for them while the friend and his contacts worked to locate and investigate Sid Harkness. Jess's friend also knew that the cruise, by its relaxing and educationally stimulating nature, would provide his friend, Jess, with a much-needed time of relaxation and reflection to help him to come to terms with the tragic loss of his wife, Allison, and their daughters. It would also be significant in refocusing Jeremy on the things in life that a young man of his age had the right to experience. Jess had been helpful through the years to the investigative agency his friend led. Together, they had uncovered serious fraud in some mortgage transactions a few years back. He had great respect for Jess and his family, and he would help in any way he could.

Jeremy was very hungry. He smelled something cooking that was surely a pot roast. He could picture it on a platter – perfectly prepared roast beef with little browned potatoes, carrots, and onions swimming in a delicious gravy. He also smelled the cinnamon and spice of an apple pie baking. He thought if he tried to picture that he would surely fall over on the floor unconscious … he was that hungry.

Jess didn't even seem to think of food at all. He just sorted quickly through all the papers and put everything in order.

Then he stood and put most of the files in his briefcase. With that, he motioned to Jeremy to follow him, patted his friend on the back, rubbed Barry behind the ears, and within moments they were in the Subaru and headed down the road and out of the gate.

They had driven for about three hours, when the new phone rang. Jess pulled over and answered it. He listened, looking serious, and then hung up.

Jess had just learned that Sid was missing. There had been an emergency at the mortgage company. No one was able to reach Sid by phone. He had not told the staff that he would be away on a camping trip, so the office manager went to look for him at his apartment. When the building manager unlocked the door, the apartment was found to be stripped bare. Sid was gone without a trace. His car was missing too.

Jess sighed and thought to himself, "This may make our lives pretty dangerous for a while." The thought crossed his mind that Sid might be out looking for them, but he quickly dismissed it as unlikely. "Someone from the past may have tracked him down, Jess mused. "That will give us a little more time," he thought. "It's a good thing we have our plans in place."

Jeremy was obviously still weighing the choice between running away from Jess and staying with him. Jess was torn between wanting to comfort and reassure the boy and the urgency of getting away, getting out of the country and not getting involved in the nightmare of the situation that was rapidly unfolding. Jess was well aware that Sid had been rumored to have done terrible things to innocent victims and had always been known to cover his tracks with money and favors. Somehow, his luck may have run out. Chances were that his disappearance was not the result of a freak accident in the forest. That would not explain the empty, stripped-down apartment and the missing car.

Jess decided not to tell Jeremy what he had just learned. The boy had been hurt so deeply in this and in previous situations in his life. Jess would have to hope that Jeremy would recover gradually from being separated from the man he had imagined was in love with him. To give Jeremy the update on Sid would serve no constructive purpose at this time. It would be better to wait until there was more information and to reassess at that time whether to pass the information along to Jeremy.

Jess knew that he should stop at a diner to get Jeremy something to eat. That was a necessity. It had been many hours since either of them had eaten anything. He saw lights ahead at a truck stop, pulled in, bought gas, and once again asking Jeremy to wait in the car, went into the diner.

Jeremy realized that if he was to run, this would be his last opportunity. He could run into the diner and immediately arouse a group of sympathizers to his cause by screaming that he was being kidnapped. The situation, he immediately realized, was almost laughable. He would be surrounded with a group of super protective, burly truckers ready to do battle for him against the one adult who had shown compassion and genuine respect for him in recent years.

Instead of flinging open the door, he reached over and pulled out the brochure Jess had placed in the console between the front seats when they had gotten into the SUV as they were leaving the ranch. It described the wonders of a world cruise to places he had read about in school but that he had never dreamed of actually seeing. If the need arose, there would be plenty of chances to find protectors on a well-run ship, he decided. Right now, he was starving and his only urgent thought was to get something to eat.

Jess came out with two good-sized bags of food and some bottles of water. It would not do for a middle aged man and a young boy to be seen together late at night at a truck stop. He drove away quickly. Bathroom stops were out, too. They would have to relieve themselves in the shelter of trees along the highway. It was still a three-hour drive to where they would leave the car in the New York City area. It would take another hour to conceal the car and then there would be the two taxis that would take them in a roundabout route to the pier in New York.

The cruise ship would be the least likely and the least conspicuous way to travel. Jess realized the risk he was taking in allowing Jeremy to go with him. But it was just too dangerous to Jeremy to have him stay anywhere in the United States until they found Sid and uncovered whatever he was up to. Jeremy was not on anyone else's radar. He had no family, and he was not under the scrutiny of law enforcement.

Jess's friend had somehow run across a late cancellation and had been able to book separate mid-ship cabins for them. This would ensure that there was little chance of seasickness, as this was the most stable section of the luxury cruise ship. Wealthy people travelled this way all the time, so they would not arouse suspicion by travelling together. Wealthy grandfathers and uncles took young relatives on these upscale cruises to further their educations.

His friend would also contact Jess's parents to let them know that Jess was safe and doing some work for him. Wade and Mary had become accustomed to this over the years. They would see that Jess's house was overseen in his absence. They would contact Allison's parents, who were also aware of the role their son-in-law had sometimes filled, in the past, in a highly confidential capacity.

Chapter Twenty-nine
On Board and Really Alive

Jeremy kept looking at himself in the cabin mirror. At first he saw a stranger and then as he looked intently into the deep blue eyes that gazed back at him, he saw instead the person he had always wanted to be. He was neatly dressed in his new khaki Dockers with a dress shirt and a blue blazer.

He couldn't help smiling. He was here with his "Uncle Jess," and he was actually safe. The effect of just thinking that word was powerful. Safe – it meant so much. He was no longer conflicted about his relationship with Sid. He was developing a healthy fear of Sid, and that in itself was a relief. He was realizing that he had been led down a dark, dangerous alley. He had been told that night was day and vice versa. He had, in short, been lied to and abused. He saw this clearly. Occasionally Jeremy would still have flashes of longing for the physical contact he had shared with Sid, but he was able to shine the light of reality on these daydreams and realize their flaws. He wanted to be the person he was meant to be. He was determined to find out who that was. He sank down on the side of his bed for a moment, looked out the patio doors, and saw the harbor. Soon the huge ship would be launched, and he would be part of the adventure. He sat up straighter and smiled. His heart beat rapidly in anticipation!

He turned his attention to the cabin. It looked like a fancy hotel room you would see in a TV show. There were two full-sized beds with four pillow each and down comforters. A desk was built into a little alcove near the side of one of the beds. It had outlets for a computer and printer. Around the corner from the desk there was a leather couch with a footstool and coffee table. All of the pieces of furniture matched. Just beyond the couch, at the far end of the room, were the sliding doors that opened onto a tiny patio with a view of the harbor. The dresser was built into a curving counter with a polished top that went all the way from the patio doors down the length of the wall and ended across from the bed. Bolted to the dresser, facing the bed, was a large-screen TV. The room was part of the dream that Jeremy was now living, he decided. Growing up, he had never had his own room, and he had never even dreamed of having such a remarkable gift!

In one of the foster homes where he had lived for a couple months when he was about 8 or 9 years old, the people had taken him to Sunday school. He thought of it now: "Thank you, God." The words were out of his mouth before he realized it, and it was a complete surprise to him that he meant what he had said!

Jess, meanwhile, was very much occupied with keeping them safe.

He had checked on all the details of the voyage and on the days and times they were expected to dock at each port. They were booked in first class cabins but not in the Premier first class. These were the cabins that had miraculously become available due to a last-minute cancellation. This was also the safest for them and would avoid putting them in a spotlight. Jeremy had been provided with appropriate clothing and with textbooks. Jess would make sure that he was seen studying every day as would any student taking a semester off from high school. Through friends, he had established Jeremy as a correspondence student at a Midwestern high school. He had obtained the textbooks and the assignments would come by email and could be viewed, completed, and sent back via internet that was now available at the major ports. That had been the easy part!

Jeremy would keep his own first name, but the documents he now carried identified his birth name as Jeremy Cook. J. Cook would be written on his homework assignments. Jeremy was not in contact with any family members. In fact, he probably had none. The mystery of what had happened to Sid troubled him, but he would have to let that go for now. He and Jeremy were safe on the ship. Jess knocked on Jeremy's cabin door. When Jeremy came to the door, Jess didn't enter the room. He just asked, "How about going up on deck to watch as we cast off and go out to sea?"

"Sure, Uncle Jess," the boy answered. He quickly put on his shoes and bounded toward the door. Jess smiled in relief! It would take time, but Jeremy was going to be all right.

The ship glided smoothly from her berth with a few mellow soundings of her horn while a band played. The captain came on the PA system and welcomed the passengers and reminded everyone to report to their assigned stations for the safety drill. He invited them to enjoy the evening, including the show in the theater, and said the casino would open as soon as they were in international waters.

After the safety drill, Jeremy and Jess went on one of the elevators to look at the gym and the spa. Then they went to look for the Grill restaurant where they would be dining. On the way they passed tastefully decorated lounges where people were sitting and talking quietly in small groups or playing cards. To Jeremy, it was a whole new world, and he felt a little lost in it. He decided he would just have to watch Uncle Jess and follow his lead.

"Let's look at the itinerary," Jess suggested. They sat in lounge chairs on deck and looked at the booklet that contained the colorful photos of exotic ports in all parts of the world, along with descriptions of the highlights of each exploratory side trip. The ports were all of interest to Jeremy. He decided that maybe he was in Heaven and whether or not he deserved to be there, he was going to enjoy himself before whoever was in charge of these things changed his mind. After spending about half an hour looking through the port excursions, they decided to go to their dining room. The first-class dining rooms had no "shifts." Diners could come in and sit down at their assigned tables at any time between 5:00 and 7:00 in the evening. If one wanted to dine at another time or in the cabin, the meal could be ordered through room service.

Chapter Thirty
At Sea

Jeremy was so hungry he could eat anything! They had found fruit and crackers in their cabins when they arrived. Jeremy devoured his in the first 15 minutes. They found the dining room just as the velvet rope was being pulled aside from its brass stand and diners were beginning to file in and look for their assigned tables. Jeremy and Jess found their table for 8 and Jess was pleased to see that it was directly across from a wide window with an excellent view. Their tablemates were an older couple from Toronto, Canada; two middle-aged sisters from Adelaide, Australia; and a couple who operated a farm near Hobart, Tasmania.

As they looked over the menu and began to get acquainted, they discovered that none of their tablemates was going to be on board for the entire cruise. Janet and Charles Norton from the Toronto suburb of High Park North had been on the ship for the Atlantic crossing from Southampton to New York City and would leave in Fort Lauderdale to board a Caribbean cruise. The sisters, Mary and Enid Sanders, would disembark in Sydney and Margaret and John Webster from Tasmania would travel as far as Auckland, New Zealand.

Jess chatted with Margaret and John who said they raised berries on their farm and also a variety of fruit trees. They had been farming there for 40 years and were taking a short holiday before the peaches would be ready early in February. They were going to disembark in Auckland, visit family there and then go home. Everyone introduced themselves, including Jeremy.

The menu offerings were amazing to Jeremy. He didn't know what some of the things were. He would ask Uncle Jess privately later. Roasted Pequillo pepper, Tuscan chicken confit salad, Game pate en croute with Cumberland sauce, asparagus and cream cheese terrine. These were total mysteries to him. He decided to order very little in spite of his hunger. Uncle Jess had warned him that he might feel a little seasick for the first day or two at sea. He decided on baked fish with French fries, green beans, and a Coke.

Jess ordered a steak and a large salad and coffee. The food was excellent. The tablemates discussed the evening program that would be featured in the theater. The sisters from Australia declared that they wanted to play poker as soon as the casino opened. Everyone was feeling relaxed.

The next port was Fort Lauderdale, which meant a leisurely voyage down the eastern coast of the U.S. without any pressure to plan for land tours unless someone wanted to ride an airboat through the Everglades.

Jess was grateful for this extra U.S. port on the itinerary in case they needed to buy clothing or other items that might not be easily obtainable in foreign ports. It was just easier to do some things while they were still in the country. The days at sea were restful. And as it turned out, there was no sea sickness. Jeremy took to the sea like the proverbial duck to water. He was able to give full range to his hearty teenage appetite. Their days fell into a comfortable rhythm. Jeremy played basketball on deck regardless of the weather. He worked out in the gym, observing the rule of doing so under the direction of an adult, as he was under the age of 18. This was fine for both of them. They fell into an easy, relaxed way of interacting – exactly as an uncle and nephew would. The weather was getting warmer every day as they moved south along the Atlantic seaboard. The January wind had a little bite to it, but it was not as cold as it had been the day they left New York harbor.

Jeremy began working on some of his assignments in algebra and English composition. Jess offered to help with anything, but admitted that science and math were his strong points. Jeremy gave Jess his English essay to read; Jess noted that it was very well written.

They attended a magic show that they agreed was not bad and a musical performance that was much better.! Jess was brooding less and enjoying life more as his anxiety eased. He had thought that Sid might try to reach him and was relieved that he had not. He wondered if anyone would look for Jeremy. The boy seemed to have no family connections or friends whatsoever. He decided to ask.

Jeremy admitted only to having had parents. "My old man was a drunk. My Mom threw him out when I was about six. When she ran out of money, they put me in foster homes, but she got me back in a few months. She got cancer and died when I was fourteen. I just stayed on at the apartment until I ran out of money. I couldn't earn that much, so I just left and started sleeping on my friends' couches and paying a few dollars here and there. I only had a few friends so I ran out of couches pretty quick. My Dad used to get drunk and beat my Mom and me, so I never looked him up. I heard he died about a year ago. "

"Did you have any brothers and sisters?"

"Nope. Just me and Mom. Mom had a sister but she died young in a car accident."

"Well," Jess said, "I guess I don't have to look for anyone to tell them about our cruise."

"No, I've been on my own for quite a while."

Jess decided not to ask how Jeremy had gotten involved with Sid until another time. Jeremy's and Jess's initial meeting had been when Sid had asked Jess to pick Jeremy up at school. There had been no explanation as to Sid's and Jeremy's relationship, though Sid had referred to Jeremy as his "nephew." That conversation could wait.

Chapter Thirty-one
Paradise and Ports of Call

The ship was a wonder to Jeremy. He explored it from top to bottom. One of the crew members showed him the crew quarters. It was amazing to him that the crew members were content to live in those tiny rooms with no view – and in bunk beds! The rooms were not much bigger than the cells at the jail. Life at sea as an occupation was hard, he decided.

In three days they reached Fort Lauderdale. They did disembark and take a tour of the Everglades in an airboat. They did some shopping to buy some things they needed. They bought swim trunks and some more clothes for the formal evenings that were coming up soon. Jess bought an extra phone to have as a spare in case he needed it. He bought a printer and a good laptop. He also bought some blank discs on which Jeremy could save his homework. From the discs, the assignments could be sent to his teachers via computer at internet cafes in the larger ports. They certainly didn't need to buy food, but they did buy a couple cases of soft drinks as they were not included with the meals and were a costly extra if purchased on the ship's beverage tab system. Coffee, tea, milk, and water were not considered extras.

It did Jess's heart good to see Jeremy enjoying the abundant, expertly prepared food served at every meal. He knew the boy had not had the luxury of a balanced diet for many years, if ever. Some people rented cabins for life on their favorite cruise ship and just lived there. He could see how that was possible. It was certainly a way to live out one's retirement worry-free if one could afford it.

The ship put out to sea two days after their arrival in Fort Lauderdale, and the carefree life at sea took hold again. It was so pleasant and energizing to greet the dawn on deck where a trainer led exercises and tai chi.

Over the next four months, the cruise took them to ports around the world. Each port provided a rich learning experience. The shift in focus from matters that had consumed their emotional space on land to the easy rhythm of the sea and the wonder of the ports of call, changed the outlook of both Jess and Jeremy. Excerpts from their travel journals reflect this gradual shift and the transformation of both travelers.

Highlights from the Journals at Sea of Jess and Jeremy

January 20, 1997 (Jess's Journal)

After breakfast, Jeremy went on deck to shoot baskets, and I, for some reason, felt compelled to go to the theater for the church service which was led by the Captain. I felt Allison's presence and sensed a wide smile on her part … imagine me going to an Episcopal Church service when it wasn't even our wedding day! It really was good to hear the old, familiar church hymns that I remembered from the times that she would convince me that it would be a beautiful experience to go to the church where we were married … Couldn't help tears coming suddenly during the second reading. It was not the "authorized Scripture passage of the day" but instead was a poem speaking eloquently of what one would do if they knew it was the last day they would be with a person for whom they cared deeply who would pass on to heaven suddenly and unexpectedly during that night.

I pictured Allison and me holding each other and saying goodbye with our daughters on our laps looking up at us with love. I think that was the picture that Allison – so present in Spirit – was drawing for me. It gave me such peace.

After the service, I went up on deck and brought Jeremy in for the lecture in the theater about our next port of call, Salvador de Bahia in Brazil.

January 21, A Day at Sea (Jess's Journal)

I made some arrangements with the Board Room concierge for transportation from the port to and from Costa Azul. After lunch, I began to look through a treasured photo album that I had stuffed carefully into my luggage as I dashed around packing the day of our unexpected departure. It was something that Allison and I had put together to record pictures of the children at various stages of their development. In one selection, Gail was pictured in front of our fireplace, reciting "The Night Before Christmas." I remembered that Allison spoke with her after the presentation about Christmas, etc. Sarah was pictured in her high chair beaming and speaking her first words. I remembered so vividly the sounds that approximated "bye," "mama," and "dada." Each section of the album advanced their age by months or years. Allison and I read to the girls, and I remembered their comments. We had talked to each other about various holidays and the plans we were making. The girls chimed in at various points. The album is a treasure that holds such poignant memories of Allison, Gail, and Sarah and of our love and joy in being together. It is beautiful, but it is bittersweet. I marked the place and will return to it later when I find the strength to imagine the sound of their voices again. I sat out on the patio and felt the peaceful rhythm of the sea after that, and I thought of Allison and felt her stroke my hair so gently that it could have been a breeze. Except for the fact that there was no stirring of the air. All was calm and quiet.

January 21, A day at sea (Jeremy's Journal)

I am learning to love the motion of the sea. So far, it has been calm and peaceful, but the captain says we will be in rough water sometimes. I think that will be fine, too.

I like the way the days go by, without any pressure to be somewhere or to do something. We can choose to do many things or do nothing. This morning I just sat in a chair on deck and closed my eyes and listened to the sounds of the ship and of the sea.

A couple times I drifted off to sleep and thought I would wake up and find Sid there. I woke up actually scared and was so glad that it had been a dream. I was so fooled by him and his lies. Tears still come to my eyes, though, when I think of how he tricked me into thinking he loved me.

January 26, Rio de Janeiro (Jess's Journal)

It was an interesting day that started with an excursion to the city center to tour the gem displays and to learn about the mining operations required to obtain these. We walked briefly on the beach made famous by Stan Getz's rendition of "The Girl from Ipanema" As we walked, I found myself telling Jeremy about Allison and my daughters. I don't know why I started talking about them, but it just seemed right. Allison nudging me, no doubt. This reminded Jeremy of his mother and her fatal illness when he was fourteen. He poured out the sad story and tears were back in my own eyes. What a tragic life this boy has lived so far. Suddenly, when he got to the part of the narrative where his mother died and he had to go alone to the funeral home and tell the undertaker, he stopped talking. That was just more than he could stand. I thought of all the loving support that surrounded me the day Allison died, and this led to more tears.

I asked, "What happened after that, Jeremy?" We had stopped walking and were looking out at the clear blue water.

"Well, they sent for the coroner, did an autopsy and said she died of cancer throughout her body. They placed her in a box that was probably made of cardboard and buried her in a far off corner of the cemetery. No one came to the burial except the man hired to dig the grave and me.

"And then I just stayed in the house until there was no electricity and no water, and even then I stayed for a while and carried water in pails. But I had no money. I heard some of the guys at school talking about getting money at a gas station, and I went along. I got $3.25 but the cops caught us afterward and arrested us. That's when I met Sid. He told the judge that he was my uncle from somewhere in New York State. I don't know how he heard about me, but there he was with papers that he said showed he was my uncle. The judge was glad to get rid of me, I think. So that's how I met Sid, He drove me to Maryland to live with him. There were others, too, that were being 'rescued.'

I rested my arm briefly across Jeremy's shoulders and felt his muscles relax. We looked at each other and nodded. I said, "Don't ever forget your Mom, Jeremy. She was a good woman who was handed an impossible job, but she made the best of it. So did you. Nothing in her hard life was your fault. Let's make her more proud of you than ever, every day!" Jeremy smiled through tears, and I did too. We turned and walked along the beach to the street.

January 26 (Jeremy's Journal)

At the gemstone museum in Rio, Uncle Jess looked at some of the jewelry in a little private room. He had a necklace made for his Mom and a little train with a jewel for a headlight for his Dad.

He told me a little about them and about how it was to grow up in a cozy little house near the railroad tracks. They sound like great parents. His Dad let him ride in the cab of a diesel engine when he was a little boy. His family had free passes to ride a Lehigh Valley Railroad train anywhere they wanted to go. They didn't have any money to spend on vacations, though. They took a ride to New York City once, and then waited at the platform in the station for the train back home and didn't go outside at all. They were afraid they would get lost and miss their train, he said.

He also bought a chain with a diamond on it for his mother-in-law and a tie clasp with a very small diamond for his father-in-law. While we waited for these to be made, we walked to the Ipanema Beach. Uncle Jess told me about his wife, Allison and his two little girls, Gail and Sarah. He hadn't said a word about them before, in all the time I've known him. He loved them so much. He had tears in his eyes when he told me about them. And so did I.

We walked along for a while after that without saying anything. It made me think of my Mom. She was so beautiful. Her name was Florence. She was tall and thin and had light brown hair that she wore in a ponytail. She was always throwing it back over her shoulder. Her hands were red from working so hard cleaning people's houses. I used to think she didn't like me because she was away from home so much. How could I have been so stupid!

I found myself telling Uncle Jess about her as we walked on that beach with all those rich people sitting on the sand with their little tents – cabanas, Uncle Jess called them.

After she stopped drinking, Mom kicked my Dad out. She was working hours and hours to make my life the best it could be. When she got sick, there was nothing we could do. There was no money for a doctor. I was 13 and I tried to get a job, but we lived in a small village in upstate New York and there was nothing. She was only sick for three months before she died. She tried to do house cleaning, but she was too weak. I would go out and take some vegetables from people's gardens in the night, but she couldn't eat them. I boiled them in water and fed her the soup. Sometimes I would find a bone or some scraps of meat in the garbage bin back of the grocery store or an old loaf of bread. Then we would have a feast.

That soup was all she ate for those last months and then she couldn't keep anything down, so she just stopped eating. She would smile and tell me that she would be all right. I kept going to school, but it was hard to study. I was always hungry. I was always worried that I would go home and find that Mom had died. I sat by her bed most nights and helped all that I could. We had no relatives and we always kept to ourselves. Mom believed in not broadcasting our business to anyone else.

She died early one morning after I had kissed her goodbye and told her I loved her. I walked down to the undertaker and told him that she had died of cancer and that she had an insurance policy for her burial. I showed it to him.

I stopped talking to Jess then and thought about that day. We walked back to the store, picked up the gifts, and were taken back to the ship by a private car service. We were both pretty quiet on the ride back.

January 27 Iguazu Falls (Jess and Jeremy)

Jeremy: We were transported to an amazing hotel inside the park that appeared quite conventional and nondescript from the front, but had a spectacular view of the Falls from every room. We had separate, very comfortable accommodations and a great breakfast in a dining room with a panoramic view of the Falls.

Uncle Jess: During that overnight stay, I thought back to the horrible days following Allison's accident when I learned that the trucking company whose driver had crossed lanes and hit our car was willing to immediately pay $20 million to settle the case out of court. I was angry at first and told Allison's father, Bill, that they were sick people to think that there was a price they could put on the lives of Allison and our daughters. Bill got me to calm down and advised me to settle. "I don't want their money," I insisted. "Yes, you do," he patiently replied. "That's the money that Allison wants you to use to do something of great consequence for someone else." I relented, and the money has been carefully invested with enough in a regular savings account to have available for sudden emergencies. It is from that fund that I am drawing now to redirect Jeremy's life. I am so grateful for the opportunity.

February 2, Day at Sea (Jeremy's Journal)

Today we learned the story of Charles Darwin and HMS Beagle. Beagle was the name of the ship that Charles Darwin was to take from England to his explorations near the tip of South America.

At breakfast, we were talking with our tablemates from Tasmania, Margaret and John, and they said Charles Darwin was a scientist who was appointed as the official naturalist on a ship named HMS Beagle that sailed from England in 1832. The captain was named FitzRoy and his job was to survey and draw accurate maps along the coast of South America so that a trade route could be set up. Darwin was a young scientist who had just graduated and was hired for this adventure to gather samples of plants and animals for study by scientists in England. He also intended to gather specimens that could be displayed in the museums in England.

It turned out that HMS Beagle followed almost the same route as our ship, stopping at Salvador Bahia, Brazil, at Rio de Janeiro, and at Buenos Aires and Montevideo.

Darwin later wrote that he hated the practice of the islanders owning slaves to run the plantations. He did not believe in slavery. He said that the people who were sold as slaves were treated very badly.

John said Charles Darwin climbed all over rock ledges and rock faces and explored every possible place where plants and animals could be found. Darwin collected many specimens of rocks and tropical plants that were not found in England. He also sent back examples of beetles and small animals from the sea. All of the bottles containing these specimens were carefully numbered and catalogued.

On the way to Montevideo from Rio our ship was led by hundreds of porpoises.

Darwin also found parts of the skull and teeth of a huge rodent, bird skeletons that had never been seen by the Englishmen, and many unusual fossils. As they went to new places, Darwin found different animals and plants in each. He was beginning to develop a theory that animals and plants were able to change and adapt to different environments. He did not use the word "evolution." That came in later years, but the term was not used by Darwin.

Darwin's ship also mapped the Strait of Magellan and saw snowcapped mountains and blue ice in the form of glaciers.

The lesson given by our friends at breakfast was worthwhile because this was the day we were to pass (as HMS Beagle had, long ago) around Cape Horn and Horn Island at the southernmost point of the continent of South America.

It is there that we would come into Drake Passage which is the Antarctic Strait that connects the Atlantic and Pacific oceans. Storms, strong ocean currents, and icebergs make this passage dangerous.

We bundled up and prepared to spend most of the day on deck, so we wouldn't miss any of this.

This is the way to learn history and geography! I love it! I still can't believe that I'm really doing this!

Note: Uncle Jess said today that maybe we could write parts of the Journal together. I'm thinking about it.
J. Cook

February 3 (Jeremy's Journal)

Note: Uncle Jess and I have decided that the rest of the Journal we will do together. We both started this adventure with so much sadness, for different reasons. We have been with good and caring people as we traveled, and we are happier now. We are ready to have friends again, to smile more, and even to laugh. We think that we can write this Journal together.
We have become real family.
J. Cook
J. Sampson
Well, here goes!

February 4 and 5 Sea Days (Jess and Jeremy)

A strange thing happened. We went to the theater for a lecture by a geologist on some melting of glaciers in Antarctica. We also learned about the possibility of something called global warming. Just as he put up his first slide, the electricity went off all over the whole ship and the lecture had to be cancelled.

February 15 Day at Sea (Jess and Jeremy)

Jeremy: Well, today is our last day before our lost day when we cross the International dateline. Uncle Jess and I sat out on deck after we worked out in the gym and he told me about his childhood. I have asked him to write it here.

Uncle Jess: Well, Jeremy, I didn't intend to publish it for the whole world to read. I am assuming that your Journal will reach a wide audience! But OK, I'll write it down.

My Mother was 32 and my Father was 35 when I was born. They had been married for 10 years, and they had begun to think that they would not have children. Dad worked for the railroad, and he worked hard. He had worked up through the ranks and had finally become a Station Master. They were proud of that. Mother had worked for a few years at Woolworth's Five and Ten Cent Store. She had been able to stop working, to be a full-time housewife when Dad was promoted. They were very careful with their money, and they didn't leave home much. I told you earlier about their free train trips.

As I said, we lived in a cozy little house with two bedrooms and one bathroom. I went to regular public schools and played basketball and hockey. While I was in High School, I was lucky enough to get a scholarship to Cornell. My first degree was in engineering and then I went for the one that was my passion; I worked for and received a Master's degree in Architecture. I had a teaching fellowship that gave me the funds for that. I loved school, but I was ready to go to work. That's how I ended up in Maryland, doing computer programming, teaching part time at Montgomery College and best of all, meeting Allison! She encouraged me to get into architecture full time. It was the right time and the right place, and with her help and accounting skills I made and saved enough money so that I can retire any time I want to. And that, up to now, is the story of my working life.

March 11 Day at Sea

Jeremy: Our plans for tomorrow in Vietnam are to go into Ho Chi Minh City on the tour bus. We will have to be up early and ready to leave on the tender to meet the bus at the port.

March 12 Vung Tau, Vietnam

Uncle Jess: We were ready to go but there was a lot of confusion at this port and the buses didn't run on schedule, in fact, our tour was scheduled for 7:45 a.m. and we were still waiting at that time. The tender takes 30 minutes to reach the port. The bus takes an additional 2 ½ hours to reach Ho Chi Minh City. By 9 a.m. only the first two tenders had left. There were hundreds of us waiting. At that point we discussed it and decided to wait our turn but to go only into the local port that was 30 minutes away. We quickly turned in our tickets for a refund and picked up tickets for the local tour to Vung Tau instead. It turned out to be an excellent decision. We had to wait two more hours, and were lucky to get good seats near a window on the tender. The heat was suffocating. We saw a tent set up to sell souvenirs as we left the tender. Then we saw our tour buses! They were old school buses that had lived a hard life. It would have been torture to ride on one of those for 5 hours into the city and back. We boarded the bus and were driven around the decaying city of Vung Tau. The city was in disrepair and there was rubble everywhere. I thought, "How could we have fought a war to try to stamp out such a poverty- stricken little place? We were driven to a "hotel," which was as dismal as the rest. We got off the shuttle and knew instinctively to step onto the other shuttle waiting to take people back to the ship. We heard later from the passengers who stayed at the "hotel" that beer was sold there at a bargain price.

At the tent, I bought some beautiful hand-painted framed paintings on rice paper showing village scenes. We were soon back on the ship. As we had suspected, those who had gone into the city were very late in returning. It was after 11 p.m., when we sailed, and the Captain was not happy because of the rhythm of the tides in that relatively shallow water.

March 31, April 1 Days at Sea (Jeremy)

Jeremy: There was an April Fool's Day spoof in the daily program. An appearance on deck by a 97-pound cat was scheduled for 10:00 a.m. He was said to be appearing with his owner Mr. Itsafake. PS – I was NOT fooled.

April 9 Last night on board the ship (Jess)

Uncle Jess: Tomorrow we will disembark at Fort Lauderdale and put into motion the plan that will hopefully lead us to Sid and the center of his operation. Tonight, we were invited to the Yacht Club Lounge for a "Cigar party." We sat outside on deck with other passengers. There was only one person smoking a cigar. We all sat and talked about the cruise and what we had learned from traveling to various parts of the world together. One of the men suggested a round of drinks combining champagne with beer, but there were no takers.

The moon peeked out from the clouds intermittently for about an hour, then apparently made a decision and fully emerged, turning the smoothly flowing sea to pure silver. I shifted my energy to blend with Allison's, and imagined that she and I held hands.

It was a magical evening.

Chapter Thirty-two
Sid's Exit

On the day he was to meet Jess and Jeremy at the campsite in the mountains, Sid stood silently in the forest, scanning in all directions. His breathing was calm and measured. He was fully confident in what he was about to do to make a needed course correction in his life. He didn't know how he could have been so careless to let that kid get so involved in his business. It was screwing up all of his careful plans. Well, if nothing else, he WAS a careful planner. The trap was laid. In a few hours, he would have a clear path ahead. He glanced quickly at his watch. They should be here in about an hour. It was his chance to get rid of a punk and an annoying "do-gooder." Who did "Uncle" Jess think he was, anyway? Jess seemed to think he was Sid's surrogate brother, but he could never be the kind of brother Sid needed. Well, the world would be better off without perfect Jess, who lived a dull life anyway and never took any chances.

Sid removed his hearing aids and placed them on top of his pack that lay beside him on the ground. They were itching as usual and distracting him from focusing on the visual field in front of and around him. He rubbed his special eye. He had to keep it sharply focused in order to perform his mission that day.

Sid had a plan for Mr. "Too Good to be True." Rumors were flying about Sid's past, and he had to stop them. Sid could easily take on a new identity and escape any scrutiny from the feds about the recent project he had set in place. The bottom line for Sid was to have a future for himself free from the bills, the debts, the bribes, the web of lies to cover his "hobby." He wanted to have freedom from it all and to start over with enough money to buy everything he craved, including the loyalty of all those he needed to own. He might ask Ross to go far away with him for a long vacation….

When they showed up, he would hit Jess first, and then take out the kid. This excited Sid, and he almost reacted accordingly. Here in his forest hideaway, he was in charge and what he had to do was almost too easy! He was tempted to laugh out loud just thinking of it.

Sid suddenly felt a change in the air, though he heard nothing. He looked up in shock and horror at the smiling, friendly face of the person in the hunting cap who was pointing a gun at him. The shot caught him completely off guard. It passed through his brain. The second was to the heart.

The hunter worked swiftly. As if the prey were a deer or bison, the body was expertly skinned and gutted on a sheet of plastic tarp and then cut into small pieces.

A pit was dug and lined with concrete. The pieces, including the entrails, were placed in the pit, covered in a lye (sodium hydroxide) solution. and buried. There would soon be no trace to identify any part of them as human remains. She had disposed of him as she had planned, as if he were a biological specimen that was no longer viable and needed to be dispensed with in a sanitary and environmentally sound way.

The forest resumed its chattering, humming, and crackling, and the hunter walked away. The hunter carried all of the deceased's personal effects in a bag, including a slice of his skull, his hearing aids, and his teeth. The next stop was Sid's apartment where Sid's key was used for entry. All traces of the dead man's life were quickly packed and removed: computers, printers, phones, papers, photos, calendars, contents of waste baskets. Nothing remained that would verify any appointments or contacts. The car was taken to a chop shop and sold. The killer waited, relaxed and confident, while the car, like its former owner, was reduced to its component parts.

Then there was nothing left to do except to wait patiently.

Chapter Thirty-three
Scales of Justice

Karen Wilson had pulled her long gray hair into a French twist and swirled it around a comb. She had put on a checked hunter's cap, pulled on her Carhartt overalls, heavy wool socks and boots, and had thrown on her hunting jacket. She had loaded her gun and put it in the holster. She was on the principal expedition of her life.

Ever since the tragic accident that had taken the light and the joy out of her life so many years ago, she had been preparing for this moment. At first, she had not known who her target was to be. She had been distraught, confused, unable to think. She had suffered what the doctors called a "nervous breakdown." She had been locked up in a lovely little private hospital for people who were insane. She had known that clearly. She had not resisted. She was too numb.

She had heard rumors about Una and David. Something terrible had happened on the day that their adopted son, Sid, had left for his job in Maryland after his graduation from Cornell. Their house had burned to the ground and they had died in their sleep. Karen had been Una's friend. But Karen had been in the hospital and helpless at that time to help Una.

Over the years, Karen had thought back to the day of Robbie's birthday party. The details that had escaped her notice at the time suddenly shot up in her memory like flames, searing her soul. She remembered Sid sitting there on the edge of the lawn near Robbie's wheelchair, not speaking, just sitting in that eerily quiet way of his. She was helping two of the children with the game. Sid's mother, Una, had taken one of the little girls inside to use the bathroom.

Her mind had gradually filled in the part she had refused to see and believe at the time. She could clearly see that strange child, Una's adopted son, Sid, reach over, undo the brake, pivot the wheelchair around and push it down the sidewalk! Somehow, she knew he had also arranged the "accidental" fire that had killed his parents. Sid was a monster! He was a danger, and he was a killer.

Those years of hospitalization gave Karen time to think through what had happened and what she must do. She had no visitors. Her poor husband, Paul, had just shriveled and died, like an empty seed pod buffeted by the wind. She had not given up, even then. She would see that justice was done and that Robbie's killer was found and punished. No one would listen to a mad woman, but she would recover fully, and she would be heard. She put all of her energetic resources into making a complete recovery so she could be discharged and put her plan into action.

Karen was finally pronounced cured and released from the hospital. She was able to go back to work on a limited basis at Cornell in the Biology department. By chance, she encountered one of the biologists who had been a department instructor when Sid Harkness had been a student. Karen raised the question as to Sid's ability as a biology student. Her colleague laughed ironically. "He was a piece of work! He was brilliant, but his passion was for dissection … He did extra credit projects in which he displayed the internal organs of small animals. He would actually hunt and kill them and then cut them into displayable pieces. It was chilling to watch. I guess he graduated summa cum laude, but he was a strange one."

That did it! Karen spoke with her department and gave notice that she would like to retire within a month. All went smoothly, she made the necessary preparations and moved to a small apartment in Maryland. She then devoted every waking hour to stalking Sid. Her father's training of her during her teenage years as a hunter gave her an advantage. Karen was a brilliant student, and she was a very practical person. She researched all of the available surveillance tools and purchased those she believed would serve her best. She went to a range several times a week for a refresher course in target practice. She was motivated and skilled. She was well prepared and had no problem waiting as long as it would take to deal with this unfinished business in her life.

Her opportunity came when she learned, by listening to his telephone conversations electronically, that Sid was going to the woods for a camping trip. She knew he was planning to take the boy, Jeremy, who was living with him, and she worried about that because she did not want any harm to come to anyone else in this criminal's life. The next break came when she heard another conversation in which Sid asked Jess to bring Jeremy to the woods. This was her one chance, and she was ready! On the day of the scheduled trip to the woods, she dressed for hunting. She recalled many happy hours in the forest hunting with her Dad during her teenage years, and how he had taught her to be an expert woodsman and a responsible hunter.

That day, she drove to the woods, and parked at a distance from the logging trail. She hiked silently to the place of meeting well ahead of the scheduled arrival of Jess and Jeremy. Her first shot did the job. The second was insurance.

Her son was free from this monster! She felt her dear little boy's beautiful spirit surround her in an affirming embrace and then float free of all earthly impediments. Una's death and her beloved Robbie's were avenged. Karen smiled gently, knowing that she had fulfilled her life purpose. She had no fear of death or retribution. When her time came, she would welcome death and the reunion with her loved ones.

For now, she would take the rest of the life-insurance money she had saved after her husband died and offer it to the Spina Bifida Research Resource, funded by the NIH Office of Rare Diseases. She would apply for permission to set up a research project which she, as a scientist and a Cornell University Professor Emerita would supervise pro bono.

Chapter Thirty-four
The Hunters and the Hunted

The ship docked in Fort Lauderdale on time, and the passengers prepared to disembark. The procedure was well organized and went smoothly. It was in order of cabin, with first-class passengers leaving the ship first. Jeremy and Jess waited their turn, and tried to be prepared for whatever they might face that day. Jess had booked a room for them at the Marriott resort in Fort Lauderdale near the Port, where he would be able to use the business center to check with efficiency on everything he needed to do.

Jeremy would be thoroughly entertained there with the beach, the pool, and the fitness center. He could also check in with his home schooling supervisor and make sure all of his assignments had reached her.

The two men who walked across the gangplank to exit the ship that day physically resembled the Jess and Jeremy who had boarded four months earlier, but there was a distinct difference! Jeremy had somehow been transformed from an awkward teenager to a confident young adult. He stood straight and carried himself with assurance. When he spoke with others, he looked at them with interest in what they were saying. He was self-assured, but sincerely polite and attentive.

Jeremy was excited about what lay ahead. He knew that the future would be of his making and that with the help of Jess and others he was on a promising path.

Jess had lost the haunted look that had crept onto his facial features with increasing regularity before the trip around the world. He would always deeply miss Allison, Sarah, and Gail, but he was increasingly aware of their living memories taking root within him and a fading of the sharpest pains of loss. It was as if they were transformed to a healing light that wrapped itself around his heart and soul. He smiled broadly in Jeremy's direction, filled with pride and affection for his nephew.

Jess and Jeremy and other passengers exchanged handshakes, smiles, and sincere good wishes.

Jess would start with his friend in Loudoun County, Virginia who owned Barry, the friendly dog. He would ask him to try to track down Sid. Jeremy had confided in him enough about Sid's activities to convince him that there were other young boys who were in danger and were being literally sold for sexual favors to some supposedly upstanding business men. This was dangerous territory, and he wanted to leave the detective work to professionals so that he would not risk any harm coming to either Jeremy or to his own family.

He made the contact, and the friend suggested that he would come to him for an in-person meeting rather than risking a phone conversation that might be overheard. The location was disclosed only via code. The next morning, he arrived, they met, and the investigation began.

Jess and Jeremy would stay where they were for the time being so that they would be as safe as possible and available for any follow-up. Sid's background was to be investigated thoroughly at the same time. There were forensic methods available now that had not been in place twenty or thirty years earlier when Sid had killed his parents and his business partner.

The call came two weeks later. The authorities had received a valuable tip from a highly respected educator who was supervising a research project for the National Institutes of Health. She had been interviewed and had given names, dates, and places of suspected human trafficking of young males in the Maryland/Washington, D.C. area. They had no idea how she had obtained this data. A detailed check had substantiated all of her findings, and subpoenas had been issued for the principals.

One of the two leaders implicated in the ring had been Sid Harkness. A piece of his skull containing an eye with an intraocular implant and all of his teeth had been found in one of the sinks in the men's room of his office building. He had been positively identified from dental records, but as there were no fingerprints or any other clues as to how they reached that destination, the case had been closed and he was presumed dead.

Chapter Thirty-five
The Last Chapter

Jess moved back to the house in Montclair to be as close as possible to the spirits of his wife and daughters among their beautiful and lasting collection of memories. Sylvia and Bill asked Jeremy if he would like to share their home, finish his senior year of high school and begin to take college courses in Manassas. He was thrilled to be part of a family and to be able to spend Saturdays with their regular guest, their honorary son, his Uncle Jess.

Plans were being discussed among Jess, Bill, and Sylvia, and Jess's mysterious contact in Loudon County, to set up a foundation that would provide a comprehensive program of healing and advanced education for the young teens who remained in the housing that had belonged to The Planning Committee. The teens would receive extensive counseling and training in computer related work. They would receive a salary immediately that would be held in trust for them and released upon their graduation from the program. They would be allowed to remain in the housing units.

The lawyers of the men who had been members of The Committee agreed to accept an out-of-court settlement on their clients' behalf that would provide income for the next 20 years to staff and to maintain the apartments. There would be renovations made to restructure the living units into suitable places for study. The teens who remained in the apartments would sign a contract accepting the responsibility of being trained to cook and maintain the unit and to enter the education and counseling program as a condition of their remaining there. The staff of each unit signed a contract to provide training in cooking and housekeeping during the period of counseling and rehabilitation.

Jess was thrilled to be able to use a generous portion of the insurance money for the purpose of setting up the foundation. Enough would, of course, be set aside for Jeremy's college education.

Jess made plans to retire and to begin a new career. It was his hope to form a not-for-profit corporation with Bill and Sylvia Myers that would provide access to legitimate rehabilitation and treatment programs for 15-17-year-old felony offenders as alternatives to incarceration. The program would initially focus on those who had been residents of rural areas. The teens' families would be included in the program to the greatest extent possible. Sylvia had contacts with a number of people who were involved in successful vocational training programs who were expressing interest in the project. She also knew of researchers at the University of Virginia who were conducting studies in the field. Jeremy was particularly interested and hoped he would be included in some way.

Jess's parents, Wade and Mary Sampson, moved into their house on Lake Montclair the following summer. It was a time of celebration and of joy.

Allison's love surrounded Jess as she let him know what she wanted most for him. It was as if she curled up next to him and whispered the words directly into his ear, as he dreamed of her and of Sarah and of Gail on a warm, starry night, "Look for love again, dearest. It's time. I'll help. Look on earth for a wife to love…."

THE END

www.ingramcontent.com/pod-product-compliance
Lightning Source LLC
Chambersburg PA
CBHW070948120726
47910CB00004B/1166